His Towel Dropped To The Floor

as he enfolded her so fiercely she thought her bones would break. She could feel his nakedness as he buried his face in her neck. For the first time she realized how Rafe's desire for her must have smoldered for years, only to blaze up when they met again. She was sure it would consume her, too. Her blood was on fire now; she was aching to unite with him.

He didn't say a word. Instead he devoured her with kisses that pressed against her eyelids, her cheeks, her mouth. A moment later his tongue was parting her lips, probing sweetly as if to offer a foretaste of his love. Mindless, she gave herself over into his keeping. All the barriers that had seemed so forbidding were crashing at their feet.

D1115319

Dear Reader,

Welcome to Silhouette! Our goal is to give you hours of unbeatable reading pleasure, and we hope you'll enjoy each month's six new Silhouette Desires. These sensual, provocative love stories are both believable and compelling—sometimes they're poignant, sometimes humorous, but always enjoyable.

Indulge yourself. Experience all the passion and excitement of falling in love along with our heroine as she meets the irresistible man of her dreams and together they overcome all obstacles in the path to a happy ending.

If this is your first Desire, I hope it'll be the first of many. If you're already a Silhouette Desire reader, thanks for your support! Look for some of your favorite authors in the coming months: Stephanie James, Diana Palmer, Dixie Browning, Ann Major and Doreen Owens Malek, to name just a few.

Happy reading!

Isabel Swift
Senior Editor

SUZANNE CAREY
Love
Medicine

Silhouette Desire

Published by Silhouette Books New York

America's Publisher of Contemporary Romance

SILHOUETTE BOOKS
300 East 42nd St., New York, N.Y. 10017

Books by Suzanne Carey

Silhouette Desire

Kiss And Tell #4
Passion's Portrait #69
Mountain Memory #92
Leave Me Never #126
Counterparts #176
Angel in His Arms #206
Confess to Apollo #268
Love Medicine #310

SUZANNE CAREY,

a reporter by training, a romance writer by choice, likes to research her stories carefully and write about the places and people she knows best. For this reason, her books have a real-life quality that intrigues readers as much as it touches their hearts.

For Laurin and Blayne Bosse, and their son,
Graydon, the best little boy I ever knew.

One

Want to dance, *gringa*?"

The words, spoken in a deeply resonant male voice, gave twenty-eight-year-old Diana Bailey an extraordinary sense of déjà vu. Sitting in the pub and restaurant of the old Weatherford Hotel while she waited for her childhood friend, Buffy Decker, she'd been mulling over the past. But she hadn't been thinking about the first time she'd heard that particular question, or the incident it had provoked at the country tavern south of town the night after her graduation from high school.

Looking up, she met dark eyes beneath level black brows, just as she had known she would. He was wearing faded jeans, a leather cowboy belt with a hammered silver buckle and a beige hand-tailored Western shirt that had definitely cost him some money. The shirt was open at the neck and it set off his coppery complexion. Rafael Marquez, she acknowledged, but didn't speak his name aloud. She had recognized him instantly, of course, though it had been almost ten years.

Not quite believing he had turned up here at the Weatherford, Diana let her gaze rest on the straight, coal-black hair that had been bequeathed him by his Indian mother. She traced visually the arrogant profile he'd inherited from his father's side. She recalled that he'd been raised on the reservation until he was nine, going to live with his father, rancher and Coconino County supervisor Joaquin Marquez, only after his mother's death. Whatever his background, it was evident that here was a man to be reckoned with. Diana couldn't pretend she hadn't thought of him over the years, or speculated about what might have happened between them if Del hadn't intervened.

Yet, in her entire life she'd spoken to him only twice—once at the age of seventeen when he'd stopped her runaway horse in one of the washes near her father's ranch, and once at eighteen when, as a newly returned Vietnam veteran, he'd asked her to dance.

It had been a chance meeting that second time, just like the first; the Alpine Air Tavern was hardly one of her usual haunts. She'd gone there that evening with friends, most of them college age, for a postgraduation fling. Giving Rafe the benefit of the doubt, it probably hadn't been clear in the crush of people that Del Cates was her escort. And she'd been too flattered and excited to explain.

Del, meanwhile, hadn't been ready to grant him the benefit of Diana's company. Jealous by nature, proud of his senior-year status at Northern Arizona University and more than a little drunk, he'd staggered up from his place at Diana's side and tried to shove Rafe around—with disastrous consequences. Beer bottles had tipped over and glasses had broken; chairs had gone flying in all directions.

She remembered drawing in a sharp, disloyal breath when Del's fist had connected with Rafe's jaw. But there had never been any real contest. After thoroughly pinning back Del's ears, Rafe had brushed himself off and apologized to her for spoiling her evening. Moments later, he'd walked out of the tavern and out of her life. Guiltily she'd tried to forget him and evince some sympathy for Del. Yet her strongest emotions at that moment had been annoyance and regret. Because of the fracas Del had caused, she and Rafe had never danced together.

Looking at Rafe now, she saw that the promise of the man she remembered seeing in him had been strikingly fulfilled. Though his build was still lithe and lean, and his flat mid-section remained almost concave above his belt buckle, his shoulders seemed broader, more powerful. There was a suggestion in his eyes, too, that by now he knew exactly what kind of man he was and what he wanted from the world.

He was not the sort that Del, drunk or sober, would care to tangle with these days, she surmised.

"Aren't you going to respond to my invitation?" Rafe prompted, a trace of what might be amusement deepening the attractive little crease beside his mouth.

"This isn't the Alpine Air Tavern," she reminded, her voice coming out a little huskier than she'd intended. "Anyway, the piano player who entertains the lunch crowd here has long since left for the afternoon."

"I wasn't sure you'd remember."

They continued to regard each other. The man-woman currents that had sparked between them at the little country bar came crackling to life again. I understand he has money now, she thought. If so, it hasn't spoiled his maverick air. Someone, Buffy perhaps, had mentioned in a letter that he'd inherited his father's considerable estate. But she knew he'd be somebody special even if he didn't have a nickel in his pocket.

"May I join you?"

Tentatively he laid a hand on the back of one of the bentwood chairs at her table. A Joan Baez song, ironic and sweet, was playing. To Diana, the whole seventies' ambiance of the restaurant—plants, exposed brick walls, historical artifacts such as an old railroad safe, and waitresses who looked as if they belonged to the Sierra Club—was a perfect backdrop for their unexpected reunion.

It's almost as if we could take things up where they left off ten years ago, she thought. The idea excited her. Nowhere, during all her time back east, had she met anyone quite like him.

"I'm waiting for someone," she replied, lightly measuring his interest.

"I'll wait with you, then."

Matter-of-factly he sat down and pulled his chair closer to hers—willing, it seemed, to brave another onslaught for the privilege of her company. Slowly he smiled at her, his teeth white and even against his coppery tan. The smile seemed to acknowledge their slight feelings of awkwardness and dispense with them. It didn't leave her with any doubt that he wanted to be friends.

He's even better-looking than I remembered, she decided, smiling back at him. I like the way those Navaho cheekbones set off his aristocratic Spanish face.

"You didn't really think I'd forget you?" she asked. "You gave my date quite a plastering."

Rafe chuckled. "Good old Del—one of our illustrious assistant district attorneys these days, or so I'm told. Is that who you're waiting for?"

"No," said Diana truthfully, as one of the waitresses approached. She was silent while Rafe ordered coffee, deciding not to tell him she'd be seeing Del at her father's house that evening. There wasn't any point in giving him the wrong impression. He'd assume she and Del were still an item, and that just wasn't so, no matter how much Del might want it to be.

They chatted a few moments more and then Rafe's coffee arrived. Bright Arizona sunlight flooded in the window beside their table, dappling his hands as he stirred in sugar and cream. "What are you doing back in Flagstaff?" he asked, regarding her over his steaming mug. "I heard you graduated from medical school. Are you going to set up your practice here?"

"Right on the first count, at least. I graduated from Johns Hopkins a couple of years ago. I've been in one residency or another ever since."

"I suppose I should be calling you *Dr.* Bailey, then."

She shook her head. "Diana's fine. In answer to your question, I plan to accept a research fellowship when I return to Maryland in mid-September."

His face registered genuine regret. "That's too bad..."

"Not really. It's something I want to do. I'll go into practice in a few years, I imagine, though probably not here. I'm in Flagstaff now because of my father. Maybe you heard, he suffered a stroke last month. I was back then, for several days, until he got off the critical list. I returned for a longer visit as soon as I could."

Her voice trailed off. I don't really know him at all, she acknowledged, though I feel as if I should. We were never friends in the usual sense. Yet I always noticed him, in a way I've never noticed any other man. Even after I grew up, I used to have the odd feeling I could count on him if I needed help or protection.

Of course, no real relationship had been possible between them. They had never moved in the same circles. Anyway, everyone knew how her father felt about Indians, even part-Indians with the looks, breeding and intelligence of a Rafe Marquez. If they'd danced together that evening—if he'd ever wrapped those strong arms around her—what might have followed could have set off the Navaho wars again, at least in her own family.

She supposed it was just as well she'd be leaving in a few weeks. She was older now and hopefully wiser. He would be a hard man to resist. And she couldn't go against her father's wishes—not with his health in such a precarious state.

"Do you stop by here often?" she asked, undeterred from wanting to know everything about him that she could.

He shook his head. "I saw you sitting there through the window, with the sunlight on your hair. I came inside just to see if it was really you."

"Well, it really is."

"I can see that, Diana."

There wasn't even a trace of irony in the words. The waitress hovered beside them to pour more coffee. As she moved on, they reached for the cream at the same moment, and their hands brushed. The sensation was electric, in direct contrast to their disjointed conversation. How warm his skin is, she thought, imagining how it might feel to lace her fingers through his. Maybe it was crazy, but there was a part of her that wanted to walk out of the Weatherford with him and go wherever he was going that sunny afternoon.

"Let me," Rafe said, the little furrow deepening again beside his mouth.

He had probably guessed at the effect he had on her composure. "What are you doing now?" she asked, keeping a casual tone.

"Running my own helicopter business. It's called Arizona Skyhook, and it's based in Sedona. I run commercial flights, take tourists up, provide backup rescue service for the DPS, that kind of thing."

"Helicopters..." Diana frowned. "Somehow I thought you'd take over your father's ranch."

Quietly he seemed to assess the extent of what she knew about his family background and find it greater than he'd expected. "That property was sold to the government, to be incorporated into the Navaho reservation," he said. "I have a small horse farm now on 89A, just above the switchbacks of Oak Creek Canyon. I guess the helicopter thing is a holdover from Vietnam. I jockeyed medics around over there for a while, you know."

"That must have been pretty grim."

He nodded. "I didn't approve of much about that war. But I was there. I had to do the best I could."

"Too bad we didn't keep in touch." Unwittingly Diana gave him a sudden glimpse of what she was feeling as she imagined him in fatigues and combat boots, with weary circles under his eyes. "I'd have written to you," she said.

One dark brow shot up a little. "Just because I caught up with you in the wash that day? You were just a scared little kid when I'd seen you last, trying to tough it out and pretend you weren't afraid. By the time I shipped out for Southeast Asia, you probably didn't even remember me."

"I remembered." She paused, searching for the right words to explain what she'd felt. "You were kind and you didn't act as if I was a pain in the neck for letting the horse get away from me," she said at last. "I remember thinking how nice it would be to have a big brother like you."

"Brother?" The single word was harsh and more than a little incredulous. "Diana..."

"Yes, I know. Stupid of me." She stirred her coffee unnecessarily. "I have to admit, I didn't see you that way at the Alpine Air..."

Rafe's face went completely serious at that. "How did you see me?" he asked.

"Like somebody I wanted to dance with very much."

She had spoken in a whisper, and this time, the silence between them was a palpable thing. Rafe laid one firm, callused hand over hers. Though her lips parted slightly, she didn't object.

"Let me tell you something," he said. "When I got back from Nam, I used to see you driving around town with your friends in that maroon convertible Del had. Your yellow hair was like a flag to me. I wanted to know if you were anything like the skinny brat I'd once grabbed up to safety in my arms."

"And was I?" Diana breathed.

"No." Pausing, Rafe lit a cigarette. "You were beautiful," he said at last, blowing out a little cloud of smoke. "I even had my own special name for you."

"What . . . what was it?"

"Cornsilk Woman," he replied.

"I hope I'm not interrupting anything."

Buffy's voice was cheerful and more than a little inquisitive as she plunked herself down at the table. Unobtrusively Rafe withdrew his hand, but not before he'd given Diana's a little squeeze. Like the secret name he'd revealed, the private gesture left her defenseless. There was no denying the powerful sexuality of this man or the unmistakable fact that at one time he'd been very interested in her.

Was he still? she wondered. Or had he come into the Weatherford merely to satisfy a half-forgotten curiosity? I suppose he has a wife or a woman somewhere, she thought, absently lifting one hand to her shining cap of Scandinavian blond hair. A man like that would hardly be without one.

Noting the gesture, he turned with ease to her friend. "Hello, Buffy," he said. "How are things in Tuba City today?"

"Hello, yourself." Buffy's square, freckled face crinkled up in a friendly smile. "The same as yesterday," she added. "But then you ought to know."

Diana looked from Buffy to Rafe and back again. "I was about to make introductions," she said. "But I see you two know each other."

Buffy's blue eyes sparkled mischievously. "Actually," she explained, "Rafe and I occasionally work together. The government hospital has a new program of TB tests, school vaccinations and other health screenings in remote areas of the reservation. I don't have to tell you what the roads are like out there. So we usually fly to our destination. Rafe is under contract as our pilot."

"That sounds . . . very interesting."

Rafe grinned. "It can be. As a physician, you might not approve, Diana, but sometimes I help out . . . thanks to my experience with the medics."

Diana didn't reply and the conversation drifted along the path of least resistance, with Rafe and Buffy talking shop and referring to people Diana didn't know. Listening to them, she observed that her friend was quite relaxed in Rafe's company. Doubtless she would know the answers to most of Diana's questions about him.

She couldn't help but wonder what Buffy's father, Max Decker, who was also her own father's right-hand man, thought about his daughter's association with Indians—particularly the handsome, part-Indian pilot. If anyone was more prejudiced against Indians than Josh Bailey, it was Max. He probably doesn't worry because Buffy is getting married in two weeks, she guessed. I don't need to be jealous of her—if jealousy is what I feel—for the same reason; she's never had eyes for anyone but Rob since we were small.

Still, Diana half resented her old chum's arrival at what had been a critical moment in the conversation. She felt as if they'd been on the brink of something, some kind of discovery about each other. Now the talk had turned trivial, and all the heady, supercharged feeling was gone. After we leave here today for our fittings, she thought, I probably won't see him again.

That wasn't how she wanted it to be as they said goodbye to Rafe at the corner of Leroux and Aspen streets.

"See you, Tuesday, Buff," he said casually, shaking hands with her friend. Expecting a similarly offhand pleasantry in turn, Diana couldn't suppress a deep flutter of excitement as he took both her hands in his. "I'm glad we had this chance to talk," he said, the earlier warmth back in his voice. "After all this time, I haven't been disappointed in you."

"Nor I in you," she replied, getting lost in enigmatic dark eyes.

Their first stop after the Weatherford was at the dressmaker's little shop in the east end of town. The measurements completed for the slim, green silk gown she would wear as Buffy's maid of honor, Diana sat back to observe her friend. Bristling with pins in her partially constructed satin and lace dress, Buffy stood before a three-way mirror. A bit chunky and plain despite her personality, she already had the happy, radiant look of a bride.

I'm glad for her, Diana thought pensively, overtaken by a certain restlessness. For the past ten years, her education and the career that was to follow it had necessarily consumed her life. Oh, she'd dated, to be sure—even briefly had had a lover or two. But in retrospect, she'd never been in love.

Now she had the strong feeling that something was missing from her life—something Rafe had reminded her of just by being the kind of man he was.

Sighing, she recrossed long, shapely legs. After the fitting she and Buffy planned to go for a swim at the Fairfield Country Club, where her father was a member. Then, there would be a crowd of people at dinner that evening—Del, Buffy, Rob and an old family friend, Senator Jack Thurston, in addition to Josh and herself. Unable to get Rafe out of her mind, she wasn't in the mood for so much company. She caught herself lightly stroking the back of one hand, reliving the moment when he'd given it that private squeeze. What I want is the chance to go somewhere alone and just think about him, she admitted to herself.

His name didn't come up immediately at the country club pool. Buffy was too engrossed with her wedding plans to mention it at first. While she lounged in one of the beige and brown deck chairs going over some last-minute lists, Diana swam lap after lap in the turquoise pool, trying to dispel her sensation of being off balance and unleash some of the caged energy she felt. Exhausted finally, she leaned her elbows on the pool apron at the deep end and stared out from beneath dripping lashes at the distant San Francisco peaks, sacred both to the Hopi and the Navaho and popular with local skiers in the winter.

Nothing will happen, she reminded herself, taking several deep breaths. You'll be here a few weeks and then go back east. Ten years from now, you'll be in town on a visit with the man you marry and you'll see Rafe again, lifting one of his kids into the back of a pickup truck.

You'll walk over and say hello, introduce your husband and recount the story of how Rafe saved you from a runaway horse when you were a child. Rafe will catch you with those passionate eyes and smile that heartbreaking smile without even realizing what it makes you feel. But even if you're contented with your life by then, you'll want to touch that little groove beside his mouth with your fingertips before you turn away.

With a groan, she thrust the imagined scenario aside and dived fiercely underwater. Swimming back to the shallow end, she climbed up the ladder and reached for a towel.

"I was wondering how you knew Rafe Marquez," Buffy remarked, putting down her list as she unerringly targeted Diana's thoughts. "Apart from what happened that time at the tavern, I mean."

With reluctance, Diana described the runaway-horse episode. She felt as if she were divulging a precious secret. "Is he married?" she asked suddenly, and then longed to bite her tongue. "I didn't notice a wedding band," she went on in disinterested fashion, vigorously drying her hair.

"No, he's not married."

The odd timbre of Buffy's voice made Diana abandon her nonchalance. Glancing up at her friend, she met a keen look of speculation.

"*What?*" she asked irritably, her forehead furrowing. "Why are you staring at me that way?"

She was half-afraid to hear the answer. Her old friend had always been exceptionally intuitive where she was concerned.

Buffy was silent a moment, assessing her. "I don't know what you're going to do about it," she said finally. "But I have a feeling Rafe Marquez is in love with you."

Two

The idea was ridiculous, of course. You had to *know* someone to be in love with them, and she and Rafe had never really known each other. The ardent and precipitous interest she felt, like his curiosity about her, could rightly be attributed to another source. Pheromones, she decided with her logical physician's brain; a chemical attraction given off by the skin.

But she couldn't discount the half-mystical tie that seemed to stem from their past meetings, or the sudden sense of incompleteness she felt. Rafe Marquez had become a powerful item of unfinished business on her agenda, whether or not that's how she wanted it to be.

"You're wrong, Buffy," she protested, shrugging on her short terry-cloth jacket. "I'm just a curiosity to him, a girl he almost danced with a long time ago."

Yet Rafe was still very much on her mind as she bathed and changed that evening at her father's town home on Mount Pleasant Road in the hills above the country club. Pausing at the oval pier glass that had graced her room since she was a child, she regarded herself quizzically. I'd like to see him again, at least once while I'm here, she thought. Even though it means playing with fire. Did I give him any hint of that? Or am I still the girl in the maroon convertible—Josh Bailey's unapproachable daughter, insulated by her M.D. degree and her Eastern connections, the same elite cadre of friends she ran around with in high school?

Standing there in a lace-trimmed peach silk camisole and matching tap panties with her damp hair spiking about her face, she didn't look aloof at all. Instead, she was the very soul of vulnerability, a woman who had begun to feel a strong attraction to a particular man, and whose lips were parting slightly at the thought of being kissed.

Josh would have another stroke if he knew what I was thinking, she admitted, hugging her bare arms. Even the slightest suggestion that Rafe's tanned, capable hands might touch his daughter's skin . . .

She couldn't deny the fantasy had a powerful effect on her as well. Blinking, she turned away from her own too-revealing gaze. It occurred to her that she had a photograph of Rafe somewhere, one she had cut from the newspaper not long after the Alpine Air incident. She remembered curling up there on the window seat in her robe and pajamas to study it with fascination.

Rummaging through the desk drawer where she kept old mementos and dance programs, she quickly

located the clipping she had in mind. Yellowing now
and a little fragile, it was a tangible reminder of the
past. "Flagstaff vet gets highest congressional award,"
the modest headline read. Beneath it was an unsmil-
ing picture of Rafe as he'd appeared ten years earlier,
standing at attention in his decorated uniform.

The brief text described a rescue he'd carried out
with his helicopter under a barrage of North Vietnam
gunfire. Seven lives had been saved as a result of his
daring. He was listed as the son of Joaquin Marquez,
Flagstaff, and the late Rose Yazzie of Indian Wells.

How intense he looked, Diana thought, sinking
down among the soft old cushions with the clipping in
her hand. It probably wasn't easy for him, growing up
with one foot in each of two widely disparate cul-
tures—three if you counted his father's Spanish
background as a separate influence. Coming back
from Vietnam with all his memories of what happened there must only have added to that feeling,
especially when he watched our silly, headless carry-
ings-on.

Back then, she guessed, Rafe might justifiably have
resented her carefree and protected existence, even if
he had been attracted by her "yellow hair." The word
gringa was usually a less-than-complimentary term for
North Americans of Anglo-Saxon heritage. She had
sensed a twist of irony the first time he'd used it—almost of disparagement, as if he'd expected her to refuse him.

There'd been no echo of that feeling at the Weatherford. Instead, he'd call her *gringa* that afternoon as
a reminder, in what she'd construed as an approving
tone. Yet the intensity is still there, though it's better
controlled, she thought. Unless I miss my guess, he's

still a man to feel things keenly; a man of strong opinions and desires.

Just then, there was a light tap at her door. Buffy entered, already dressed for dinner in a ruffly blue-and-white checked cotton dress. Hastily Diana tucked the clipping out of sight, crumpling it a little in the process.

"Not ready yet?" Buffy asked. "Penny for your thoughts."

Diana ran her fingers through short, blond hair that had begun to dry in an unruly fashion. "They're not worth much more than that," she observed with an airy approximation of the truth. "I was just remembering all the things that happened at our graduation. I guess meeting Rafe Marquez today brought it all back to mind."

Everyone, including Buffy, was in Josh's study having cocktails when she came down wearing an expensive, berry-colored silk gown that moved easily with her body. Her wayward curls had been coaxed smoothly into place, and she'd chosen the simple, perfect ornament of a heavy silver bracelet.

"Ah, Diana," her father grumbled approvingly, his voice still an authoritative bass despite the poor articulation his stroke had caused. "You look lovely tonight."

"Yes, doesn't she?" Senator Thurston asked. "Success in a man's world hasn't made you any less the woman, my dear."

Diana knew he meant the remark as a compliment. "Medicine isn't exclusively a man's province anymore, Senator," she responded mildly, giving him the expected kiss.

A moment later, she was returning Max's gruff nod and greeting Buffy's fiancé with an affectionate hug. Out of the corner of her eye, she saw Del abandon his glass on the mantel where he had been lounging beside Josh's wheelchair. Coming over, he took both her hands in his. It was the same gesture Rafe had made out on the sidewalk that afternoon. Yet this time, she felt nothing beyond the casual friendliness she'd entertained for her former date of years gone by.

"No kiss or hug for me, Diana?" he joked, standing a little too close. "It's been an awfully long time."

"Only a month." But Diana knew Del thought her whirlwind visit when Josh had been taken to the hospital hadn't really counted. She offered her cheek, letting her hands rest in his without protest. "Win any good cases lately?"

He grinned. "Actually, there was one. Senator Thurston is right, you know; you look good enough to eat. I'll try to be civilized...provided you sit beside me at dinner tonight."

"Always plea-bargaining, aren't you?" Deftly she led him back to her father's side. "You know as well as I do that doctors and lawyers are poor company... even on the golf course."

Too bad he doesn't make me feel what Rafe can without even trying, she admitted to herself a few minutes later as they walked together into the antique-furnished dining room. But he doesn't, and he probably never will. It was a shame, really. Since Del had joined the district attorney's office, he and Josh, who'd always had his finger in every political pie, had become fast friends. Barring a physician with an East Coast establishment background, Del was exactly the kind of man who would please her father best.

They sat themselves around the table with Josh, in his wheelchair, at its head. As she chatted with Del and Senator Thurston on either side of her, Diana noted that the meal being served by the family housekeeper, Mrs. Purdy, perfectly complemented her late mother's English bone china and Val St-Lambert crystal. Hinting at the elegant fare of the eastern seaboard, it paid no debt to Arizona's diverse Indian and Spanish culinary heritage.

Josh loves this place and he'd never leave it, she mused as the soup was served. Sometimes, though, it's as if he wants to turn his back on it and pretend he's thousands of miles from here.

Her father, with his shock of white hair and weathered rugged features, would eat little that evening, she knew. His right hand was still weak and his left unaccustomed to much use. Inevitably some of the food would spill. With characteristic toughness, he would ignore it and control the table talk as firmly as always.

Though the flesh now hung loosely on his tall once-powerful frame, the force of his personality was still a tangible thing. Deeply hooded, his dark-brown almost-black eyes didn't miss a nuance of expression or gesture. It was completely in character that he refused to curtail either his business or social life any more than he must.

Over the salad, talk turned to Buffy's wedding. Diana felt more than her usual slight annoyance when Senator Thurston demanded to know when she would follow suit. Lately Josh had been making similar noises, and referring obliquely to the time when he would have grandchildren, even though he simultaneously seemed a bit ambivalent about that notion.

She was trying to think of a suitably noncommittal reply when the phone rang out in the hall. Mrs. Purdy went to answer it. A moment later, her footsteps returned to the dining room.

"A call for you, Miss Diana," the housekeeper said.

Diana, who had drifted away from many of her casual acquaintances in Flagstaff over the past ten years, expressed surprise. "Who is it?" she asked. "Could you possibly take a message?"

"Mr. Rafael Marquez, Miss," Mrs. Purdy replied, awaiting instructions.

Oh, *no*, Diana thought. I wanted to hear from him. But of all the worst possible moments...

She could feel everyone staring. Meanwhile her own eyes were drawn to her father. His color had risen alarmingly and he was clenching the bony knuckles of his good hand.

"Not Joaquin Marquez's bastard?" he demanded with harsh disregard for the amenities. "Diana..."

"Josh, please!" She could feel the blood rushing to her own cheeks. Almost without realizing it, she had risen from her seat, letting her napkin slip to the floor. "We have guests," she reproached, getting control of herself. "If you'll just excuse me for a moment, I'll see what he wants."

"Half Indian," Josh mumbled. "I don't like it...."

Mortified, Diana hurriedly left the room. The receiver was lying beside the phone on the Chippendale hall table. Her spike heels clicked over red clay quarry tiles as she advanced toward it. She could hear the conversation around the dinner table awkwardly coming to life again.

"Hello, Rafe," she said softly, putting the receiver to her ear.

"I called at a bad time, didn't I?" Coming over the wire, his voice was even deeper and more suggestive of that male-animal quality he radiated than she'd expected. "If it's not convenient to talk now, you could call me back later," he said. "Shall I give you my number?"

She almost agreed to let him. But the words *Joaquin Marquez's bastard* were still ringing in her ears and prickling at her conscience. No one—not even Josh in his weakened condition—had a right to talk that way, or to make her feel guilty about being acquainted with such a personable man.

"We have dinner guests this evening," she admitted. "But I can talk for a minute or so. What can I do for you?"

He chuckled, with the rich, baritone sound she'd heard that afternoon. She found herself warming to it, despite the uncomfortable situation.

"You know perfectly well what I want, Diana," he said. "To see you again. How about tomorrow evening? Are you free for dinner then?"

Say yes, her inner self urged, even as she tried to picture him at the other end of the line. Was he calling from his business, perhaps, with the helicopter parked just outside the window of what would be his corrugated metal office? She imagined him sitting on the edge of his desk beside the phone, his long legs in the much-washed jeans stretched out before him.

In her mind's eye, her gaze flicked back up over the silver belt buckle to his lean waist and powerful shoulders, resting on the curving, sensual mouth. To sit across from him in a candlelit restaurant somewhere and drown in the black pools of those extraordinary eyes would be tempting fate. But maybe she could effect a compromise.

"I'd better not," she answered. "As I told you, Josh...my father...hasn't been too well. He'll be expecting me to keep him company for dinner. But I am driving into town to see Doc Furbish in the morning. I could meet you then."

There was a short silence, and she wondered if she sounded too evasive.

"No health problems, I hope," he said.

"It's just about my father. I'm not his physician, and I can't get the straight dope from him."

"All right. Furbish is my family doctor too. I'll meet you outside his office. What time?"

Feeling like a coward, she named an hour that was too late for breakfast and too early for lunch.

"I'll be there." He paused. "It really did something to me, seeing you again today, Diana," he admitted. "I can't get you out of my thoughts."

Coward or not, she felt compelled to honesty. "I feel the same way," she confessed in a low voice. "See you tomorrow, then, Rafe. Good night."

There wasn't the slightest hitch in the conversation as she came back into the dining room. To her relief, Josh had recovered his manners sufficiently not to ask about the reason for her call. He was sure to do so later, however, and she wasn't off the hook yet, by any means. As she slid into her place, she realized the topic of conversation around the dinner table had probably arisen from the fact that she'd been talking to Rafe. Her father, Max, Del and the senator were holding forth on the seven or eight private ranches that had been bought up by the Bureau of Indian Affairs during the past few years to be added to Navaho lands.

Though her knowledge of the situation was sketchy, Diana had heard that the Hopi reservation, which was surrounded by Navaho property like a hole in a doughnut, had been enlarged by congressional edict. At the moment, Senator Thurston was emphasizing that he had voted against the measure.

Those Navahos displaced by the change, she understood from Josh's vituperative comments, were gradually being relocated at considerable taxpayer expense to the former ranches, just north and east of her father's own enormous Double Bar B spread.

That must be what Rafe was talking about when he mentioned selling his father's place to the government, she thought. Then she winced as Josh began complaining about the increased proximity of Navaho settlements to the Bailey property.

"Know what to expect now," he predicted, his lip curling. "Indian cattle running on our land, watering at our tanks when the weather gets dry."

Max shook his head. "That ain't the worst of it. What really costs is when some Navaho crosses over to hunt rabbit and cattle get shot instead. Had another calf dragged off last week," he added for Del and Senator Thurston's benefit.

"Money out of your pocket," the senator sympathized.

"And not just pocket change, either." Del was anxious to demonstrate his solidarity with Josh, particularly to her, Diana guessed.

"You're damn right." Josh was firm. "We gave 'em half the state and they ought to be satisfied with that. Less than eleven percent of Arizona is in private hands to begin with, between the federal government, state-owned property that once belonged to the railroad, and those Indians. Got to lease most of your grazing land from government agencies to make cattle pay at all.''

Diana swallowed. The Indians had been in Arizona first. And, despite the drop in beef prices, she knew, the Bailey operation was big enough to continue turning a good profit. "You don't know who took that calf, Max," she reminded her father's right-hand man. "It could have been a mountain lion or a coyote. It's not realistic or fair always to blame the Indians."

Frowning, Buffy's father declined to contradict her. She was still his employer's daughter, after all.

Josh, on the other hand, felt no compunction to keep silent. "Hell, honey," he said indulgently, "I know you've got a soft heart. But you've been away most of the time since you were in high school. You don't know what's going on out here anymore."

"That's right, Diana." Del's voice took on the authoritative, paternal tone that always made her hackles rise. "Feeling sorry for Indians can be a dangerous habit. Not too long ago, a Navaho got tanked up at one of the bars on Santa Fe Avenue and brandished a loaded shotgun at some tourists on the interstate. Somebody could have gotten killed. You would probably have stopped and given him a ride."

She bit her lip, unable to think of a ready answer—at least not one appropriate for mixed company.

Buffy gave her a look of commiseration. "Can't we change the subject?" she asked. "Everyone here knows I work with those people every day. I find them modest and reserved. Since I probably can't change anyone's opinion, I'd rather talk about something else."

Diana felt gratitude toward Buffy and annoyance at almost everyone else as the dinner party broke up later that evening.

"Walk me to my car," Del requested as he shook hands with her father by the front door. "We haven't had a moment alone."

I'm not sure I want to be alone with you, she thought leaving the sharp words unsaid. Behaving like a gracious hostess instead, she accompanied the tall, redheaded attorney to his BMW, which was parked at the edge of the drive. But when he tried to take her into his arms, she stepped decisively out of reach.

"What's the matter, Di?" he asked, trying to see her face in the shadows. "Did I do something wrong tonight?"

Diana shrugged. "I guess you could say we disagree on some things."

"Name me two people who don't have their differences." Persistently he reached for her. "After all this time, we shouldn't let a squabble about Indians keep us apart."

"Del..." She drew her cool, medical professionalism about her like a cloak. "It has been quite a while. And I'm not a high-school girl anymore."

"What does that mean?" There was genuine puzzlement in his voice, overlapping a faintly suspicious tone. "And what did Rafe Marquez want this evening, anyway? You're not involved with him, I hope."

"That's none of your business."

Her curt answer hinted at a more complicated friendship than she actually had with Rafe. But she didn't care about that. Let Del think what he wants, she decided. And report this conversation to my father, if his ethics will allow him to stoop to that.

The next moment she felt sorry to be quarreling with an old friend. "Don't be angry, Diana," he was saying, not trying to touch her now. "You know how I feel about you...how I've always felt. I've never made any secret of it. And I'm going to do everything I can during your visit to convince you to feel the same. Okay?"

Del's affection for her was genuine, even if she was irritated by his prejudice. Instinctively she responded to it. "I guess I can't fault a man for trying," she said, lightly kissing him on the cheek. "But please, Del...don't push so hard. I'm a woman with ideas and opinions of my own, for which I'd like a little respect."

After Del drove off, she slipped back into the house as quietly as she could. But she wasn't surprised when Josh's gruff voice called out to her from the study, where he was having his nightly allotment of brandy.

"I want to talk to you, Diana."

"Let it wait, Josh, if you don't mind." She made a show of massaging her temples. "I'm still tired from my flight yesterday, and I seem to be developing a headache. I think I'll just go on up to bed."

Diana dressed carefully for her meeting with Doc Furbish the next morning, not once but several times. The various combinations of skirts, blouses and jackets that ended up in a heap on her bed had been rejected for a purpose: she couldn't picture herself wearing them for the appointment that really mattered—with Rafe.

Finally she settled on a slim beige linen skirt and a long-sleeved shirt of sky-blue silk that brought out her Nordic coloring with a vengeance. Realizing that was what she'd been after all along, she regarded herself defensively. The yellow-haired girl in the mirror is making much out of nothing, she thought. At most, we'll go for coffee. He'll ask me out again and I'll tell him . . . *no*?

A *yes* would get her in over her head far too quickly, even during the short time she planned to remain in Flagstaff. But to refuse him would be to oppose the urging of her heart. If I could just spend some time with him, without it being anything so formal as a "date," she thought. Get to know him in a setting where my father's wishes didn't weigh so heavily. I suppose that's too much to ask.

It turned out that Rafe knew exactly what would please her best.

Coming out of Doc Furbish's office, she spotted him smoking and leaning against a late-model pickup truck at the curb. He was wearing a white shirt with tan jeans, and the sunlight was glinting on his thick black hair.

He's beautifully made, she admitted, taking in the lean length of him, the latent strength that was so apparent in his broad shoulders. But she knew her attraction to him was more than just a physical one. Irresistibly she was drawn to the fierce yet protective spirit she sensed in him, even more than to his almost symbolic presence in her past and the foreign quality of his Indian and Spanish heritage.

"Hello, Diana," he greeted her, the little groove deepening beside his mouth.

She advanced to stand closer to him than she'd intended. Tossing his cigarette aside, he took both her hands in his as he had the previous afternoon.

"Hello, Rafe," she answered.

For a moment, they simply regarded each other. Then, "What did Doc Furbish have to say?" he asked. "Is your father doing as well as can be expected?"

"Better, actually." Looking up into his eyes, she felt suddenly as if she were communicating in an exotic new language that didn't require the conventional use of words. With effort, she focused on his question. "But he's not out of the woods yet," she continued. "The same stubbornness that's helped him recover more quickly than we expected also encourages him to go against doctor's orders. Now that I know just what those orders are, I can enforce them..."

Their other, wordless conversation didn't falter as she fell silent. "That's good," he answered. "I was beginning to wonder. You were in there an awfully long time."

"Sorry to be late." Though she glanced at her watch as if she'd lost track of time, she knew perfectly well just how tardy she was. She'd drawn out the conversation with Doc Furbish, her old mentor, half hoping and half fearing Rafe would decide not to wait. Then, abruptly, she'd cut short her visit and dashed from the office.

"Only a little. I didn't mind."

She found herself smiling at him, unexpectedly put at her ease despite the excited, off-balance feeling he gave her. "If you know Doc," she said, "you understand how persistent he can be. Now that he wants to retire, he's nagging me even harder about coming back to Flagstaff to take over his practice."

"Good for him. We could use a doctor like you in this town."

Diana didn't answer. Yesterday she'd told him she didn't plan to settle here. Now she felt the tiniest chink of doubt.

"Since it's difficult for you to get away in the evening," he went on, coming directly to the point, "I have another proposition. How about a hike up the west fork of Oak Creek? We could meet at my place in the pines, just above the switchbacks. There are blackberries in the canyon now. The weather should be beautiful."

It was an attractive proposal, one she was drawn to accept. There would be no one to overhear their conversation or report to her father that she was seeing an Indian. "Sounds lovely," she teased, considering. "What's the fee for your services as a guide?"

Something hard glinted in the black depths of his eyes at that, and for a moment she thought she'd offended him. Then, "My Indian grandfather taught me never to barter with a woman," he replied. "I'm inclined to risk it, all the same. If you'd like to tour the reservation with me sometime while you're here, I'd consider that ample payment."

"Done," Diana said.

Curious, she was about to inquire about his motives when he drew her lightly into his arms. Cars were whizzing by in the dusty sunlight, and people were coming and going from the doctors' offices. "Please," she protested softly. "Not here..."

It was like trying to go against gravity, or deny some ancient Navaho legend of First Man and First Woman that would inevitably work itself out with them as principals in this modern-day setting. That didn't make sense, of course; though she was very attracted to his heritage, she didn't share it.

Yet she was amazed at the deep sense of connect-
edness they'd somehow forged during their past
meetings, long ago in the stony wash and later in the
country bar—even the previous afternoon at the
Weatherford, with Buffy barging in. That bond was
an almost tangible thing as he meshed one capable
brown hand in the blond curls at her nape. With the
other, he was drawing her lower body up against him.
She could feel his warm breath on her parted lips.

"Rafe," she whispered, and shut her eyes.

A moment later, his mouth covered hers. Diana's
pulse beat like a hammer as he nuzzled gently, tasting
her first as if she were some long-deferred pleasure,
and then turning his head slightly to plumb her depths.

The kiss, which had doubtless been in the cards
since she was eleven, was more compelling than her
most erotic dreams. His tongue was vigorous and insistent against hers, boldly claiming her moist re-
cesses for his own. Yet he probed sweetly too, as if he
wouldn't yet push her beyond what she was ready to
give.

Conversely, she wanted to give him everything.
Surrendering with an almost inaudible sigh, she put
her arms around him. Her breasts, their nipples hard
with desire, were crushed against the firm wall of his
chest. Eagerly her nostrils drank in his delicious, sun-
warmed scent.

In response, he hauled her more urgently up against
him. His kiss deepened, becoming a parallel form of
lovemaking that they could indulge in fully clothed
there on the sidewalk. She could feel the hardness of
his passion pressing against her.

How I could want him, she thought. A corresponding well of desire opened in her so blatantly that the

hot ache of it spread like wildfire through her body. Never, during her few lackluster affairs, had she been so physically ready to receive a man or felt such need to grant him unlimited access.

She was momentarily set adrift when Rafe drew back a little, though he still shielded himself against her. She realized with a start that, being a man, he needed a moment for his arousal to subside there in that public place. Meanwhile he was regarding her with an odd expression. There was approval in it and a kind of recognition, too, as if he'd confirmed to his satisfaction who she was.

"Ten o'clock tomorrow morning all right?" he asked, the little line that deepened whenever he smiled quirking beside his mouth.

"For... for what?" she stammered.

"For our trip into the canyon. My ranch is on the right side of the road as you travel south. The house is eight-sided and made of cedar. There's a sign that says Marquez just over the gate."

Diana nodded, her breath still coming rapidly enough to betray the depth of her own arousal. "But I don't think we should have..."

"On the contrary, Cornsilk Woman." Rafe's dark-eyed amusement deepened. "If you must barter, make sure the bargain is sealed. That's something else my Indian grandfather taught me."

Three

They didn't have coffee together as she'd expected. But then there wasn't any need. Seventeen years after their first meeting, Rafe was going after her with everything he had and they both knew it. Without putting his request into words, he had asked for and won her permission to do just that.

She had given it, despite her misgivings about her father, because it was what she wanted, too. Besides, his choice of meeting place had seemed so right. The west fork of Oak Creek was a perfect rendezvous point. They could lose themselves beneath red rock cliffs and the dappled shade of sycamores, talk privately to the background music of water tumbling over stones.

Of course it was mutually understood that they wouldn't just talk; he would kiss her again, ravage her with that splendid mouth and more—as much more as she would permit, she guessed. For one graphic moment she pictured a bed of pine straw and leaves, deeply hidden among tall grasses, Rafe's magnificent body covering her own.

But though she'd cooperated with his kiss and agreed to meet him again, she hadn't promised to carry what was happening between them to its natural conclusion. I can't let him make love to me, she warned herself as they said goodbye. Even though I'm beginning to want that more than anything in the world.

Driving out to the ranch where Max had taken Josh that morning, she gazed unseeingly at the sparse high desert country with its golden carpet of rabbitbrush and the mist-colored mesas she'd known since she was a child. The encounter with Rafe had rendered powerless some essential center of her inner self-control. She realized that she might not be able to put a stop to what they both wanted.

Glancing in the rearview mirror, she met gray eyes filled with longing. Her mouth, imprinted by his kiss, seemed softer and more vulnerable than before.

She wondered if Josh would notice the difference. In truth, very little escaped his attention. Yet he had no basis for suspecting any change. She would distract him, launching into the details of her discussion with Doc Furbish, and restating his orders in no uncertain terms.

Meanwhile she would try not to speculate too much about what might happen between herself and the handsome, half-Indian helicopter pilot. Instead she would concentrate on coming up with a story to cover her absence that Josh could accept.

Leaving the interstate behind, she was soon stirring up an enormous cloud of dust on the bumpy, stony dirt track that led to the windmill, corrals and winter ranch house of the Bailey spread. Each time she approached the Double Bar B she was reminded how much she loved the simplicity of the land and cattle; the gleam of the quarter horses' reddish flanks as they grazed in the distance; the stark, pen-and-ink quality of the empty corrals that burst into life at roundup time; the always comforting sensation of solitude and space.

When she was small, she'd imagined herself settling on a place like this with the man she loved. She'd pictured them raising kids and horses here in juniper and pinyon country. She'd be working part-time as a veterinarian for the other ranches in the area.

Josh hadn't wanted her to be a vet, just as he hadn't wanted her to settle here, even though that meant the Double Bar B would have an absentee owner someday. With the considerable force of his influence, he'd encouraged her to go away to medical school and make her home in a crowded eastern city, to "do something significant" with her life.

Being a physician who treated people was fine with her now. She loved it just as much as she might have cared for any literal realization of her childhood dream. But she wasn't certain she wanted to leave Arizona behind forever, any more than the suddenly homesick child in her had totally discounted Doc Furbish's proposition. Maybe after the fellowship runs its course, she thought, I'll come back here and set up my practice with him.

The notion of the ranch, the man and the children, on the other hand, was too dangerous to think about very seriously. If she entertained it for more than a moment, the man ceased to be a neutral, shadow figure, and assumed Rafe's black hair, coppery coloring and knowing smile.

She arrived at the house and found Josh seated in his wheelchair on the patio, gazing off toward the pine-clad high country where most of his Hereford, Charolais and Barzona cattle spent the hot summer months. She thought she could read loneliness in his stooped posture and the pensive way one bony hand was folded over the other. Then he wheeled about at her footsteps and she found to her dismay that he was angry, not lonely, his shaggy brows drawn ominously together.

"Want to tell me what you've been doin', girl?" he demanded, his eyes hard as stone. "Or do I have to get all my news from folks in town?"

Diana marshaled her emotional resources. "I don't know what you mean," she said.

"Sure about that?"

Knowing he didn't like her to stand over him when they argued, she took one of the metal patio chairs at his side. "Who's been calling you with news about me?" she asked, her gaze on a level with his.

"The *who* doesn't matter. It's what they had to say that could break a father's heart."

By this time Diana could guess what was coming. She tried to keep her face expressionless.

"I hope to hell they were wrong," Josh went on, "when they said they saw you kissing Joaquin Marquez's bastard son on a public street corner."

Despite her best intentions Diana was furious, but she didn't dare let her own anger show. Once again Josh's color had risen. He was drawing slightly more rapid, shallow breaths. With a show of calm, she took his pulse, ignoring an effort on his part to shake off her fingers. "Somewhat high, despite all the medication you're taking," she announced. "You don't want to end up back in the hospital."

"What I want, dammit, is the truth."

"All right." She didn't know it, but her wide gray eyes were as guileless as her mother's had once seemed to him. At the moment, that didn't help her cause. "I could tell you that Rafe kissed me against my will," she admitted. "That wouldn't be the truth. The fact is, we were kissing each other. I didn't expect it to happen, but I'm glad it did."

The oath her father uttered made her wince. Her jaw tightened, and for a moment Diana's family resemblance to Josh was a striking one. "Let's get one thing straight right now," she told him. "This subject is closed if you ever call him a bastard again."

"Hell, it's the truth."

But Josh was sputtering and she knew she'd made her point. Unfortunately she probably hadn't heard the last of it. Making plans with Rafe and assuming Josh wouldn't find out about them had been living in a fool's paradise. Now her attraction for the black-haired man who had kissed her so thoroughly had become a critical issue, one that could have serious ramifications for her father's health.

Mrs. Purdy brought out a pitcher of lemonade and they didn't say anything more to each other for a moment as they thanked her for her thoughtfulness. When the housekeeper was out of earshot, Diana phrased a careful question. "I'd like to know just what the problem is—Rafe's parents not being married to each other, or the fact that he has Indian blood?"

Instantly Josh was livid again. "Don't want my pretty blond daughter making love to a Navaho," he said fiercely. "You were brought up for better than that. You could have anyone you wanted."

It had never been clear to her why he disliked Indians so much. As a child she'd just accepted the fact, though she hadn't agreed with him. She'd always felt some puzzlement. His prejudices, for instance, hadn't dovetailed with stories that her mother, Ingrid, a practical nurse, had volunteered her time with both the Navahos and the Hopi for several years before her death.

For as long as Diana could remember, Josh had never been willing to discuss Ingrid Johanssen Bailey at any length, and she'd always put that down to grief. To Diana, who barely remembered her mother, he would say only that she was beautiful, strong-headed and soft of heart. Once he'd admitted that all the light had gone out of his world when she'd died miscarrying their second, stillborn child. Then he had closed up again, refusing to discuss anything to do with Ingrid's death.

"I don't understand, Dad," she said, unconsciously addressing him by the name she'd used in childhood. "If you disapprove so strongly of Indians, why didn't you try to prevent my mother from working on the reservation the way she did?"

"Hell, I did try to stop her, child."

Something broke in her father's voice on the words. To her horror, Diana saw that his eyes had filled with tears. She was overwhelmed with the conviction that what they were dealing with was a tragedy, not just Josh's irrational aversion to people unlike himself.

"Tell me about it," she begged anxiously, one arm about his shoulders. "Please. I have a right to know."

For a moment she thought he would refuse her. Then, sounding singularly old and bereft, he answered her.

"I loved your mother...very much," he said. "She was beautiful...blond and gray-eyed, like you...and outgoing, full of life. She had a social conscience, too, and I admired that about her, though I didn't share her liberal notions. I felt so lucky to have her, you see. I would have given her anything she wanted..."

Diana waited.

"What she wanted," Josh went on slowly, "was to help the Indians. She was out here on a visit from Minneapolis when we met, and the whole thing was new to her. Health conditions were pretty poor on the reservation then, and that upset her. With her nurse's training, I guess she felt a personal responsibility to do something about it."

Struggling with the words, her father went on to relate how his beloved Ingrid hadn't been able to put her plans into action right away. Though he hadn't been eager to start a family, their love had been a passionate one, and Diana had been conceived almost at once. Her mother had stayed close to the ranch to care for her until she was nearly three years old. Then she had hired a full-time nursemaid.

"That's when she started goin' out there on a regular basis," Josh told her. "I suppose I was proud of her at first, though I didn't like her messin' around with Indians. Then the work started to take up more and more of her time, and we began to argue about that. Finally, when she got pregnant again, contrary to my wishes, I put my foot down.

"'You have to choose between them and me,' I told her. 'Them and your family. I won't have you goin' out there with that baby in your belly only to get raped by some drunken Navaho who likes yellow hair.'"

"That didn't happen, did it?" Diana whispered urgently, wounded to the quick by the way his words had parodied Rafe's admiration. "*Please* say no."

"It didn't happen." For a long moment, Josh was silent.

"What then?"

"There *was* a drunken Indian." One or two tears ran down Josh's weathered cheeks. He didn't lift his good hand to wipe them away. "Your mama gave in to my ultimatum, girl, though I know it hurt her to be controlled by me that way. Sometimes I think it was an Indian devil god that prompted her to go back there one last time, to say goodbye to those people she'd been working with."

Overcome for a moment, her father shut his eyes. "She was coming back when that Navaho plowed head-on into her little Chevy on one of those dusty, back-country roads," he finished. "She lost the baby first. And *then* she died."

By now, Diana was weeping too. "I never knew," she whispered hoarsely, leaning her head on her father's shoulder. "How awful that must have been for you, losing them both just when you thought they would be safe."

"It was hell. If it hadn't been for you, girl, I wouldn't have had much reason to keep on going in this old world."

For a while they just sat there in silence, Diana willing with all her strength that the comfort of her presence would be enough.

"What happened was terrible," she said finally. "And I know that kind of thing still goes on sometimes, like the incident Del described to us last night. But not all Indians get roaring drunk and smash into people. Most wouldn't dream of it—even if laws forbidding them to have alcohol on the reservation didn't leave them with just two options, not drinking or drinking in town."

"Maybe not." Josh's face was clouded, almost ashen now with weariness. "But all it took was one, and Ingrid and her baby were gone. I beg you, girl…don't get mixed up with the Marquez boy. Don't want any black-haired Indian brats around here to remind me of what I lost."

Diana was torn the next morning when she lied to her father at breakfast, saying that she planned to meet a friend for some shopping in Sedona, and then drove off to meet Rafe. The story of how her mother had died had left her shaken, though she didn't share her father's animosity for the Navaho he said was responsible. But the still-jagged emotions that had accompanied his tale left her more sympathetic to Josh's viewpoint, even if she couldn't subscribe to it. More than ever, she realized that to get too involved with her handsome part-Indian suitor could destroy her relationship with Josh, if not also ruin his health. Guilt had prompted her to pick up the phone more than once with the idea of canceling their outing, but further reflection had convinced her that wasn't her style.

Now, slowing the progress of her father's Wagoneer at the gate of Rafe's ranch, she knew in her heart how much she had wanted to go ahead with the plan. Framed by pointed ponderosa pines at the end of a rose-red volcanic cinder drive, the cedar house perfectly matched the man she was beginning to know. With a raised deck that overlooked the paddock, corrals and barn, it was octagonally shaped, like a very large modern hogan that had been designed by an architect. Stone chimneys bespoke several large fireplaces. Sun reflected off a skylight that would afford a man used to the freedom of the Arizona skies a chance to contemplate the stars.

Rafe himself was visible at the barn. Waving a casual hello, he continued to saddle up a pair of sleek riding horses while she parked her father's vehicle by the fence.

"I thought we might ride down," he said as she approached, his black eyes glinting at her. "It isn't far. Of course we'll have to tie up the horses before we cross over to Mayhew's Lodge."

The dizzying descent down the Oak Creek switchbacks was far more breathtaking than she'd remembered. They rode single file because of the traffic, Rafe leading the way with erect, easy grace. The plunging blue-green vista of pines, canyon walls and distance seemed to urge that she forget caution and open herself to whatever experiences the morning would provide.

Before long, they were leaving the highway at the entrance to the west-fork trail and tying up the horses. "C'mon," said Rafe, slinging a canteen over his shoulder and holding out his hand to her.

She let him lace his fingers through hers. Laughing at each other, they crossed a rough plank that tipped alarmingly and threatened to spill them into the stony-cold water of Oak Creek. Briefly they paused to explore the ruins of Mayhew's Lodge, where writer Zane

Grey had once lived after penning his famed *Call of the Canyon* upstairs at the Weatherford.

Then they were picking their way along the boulder-strewn fork itself in the slanting sunlight under a lush canopy of sycamore and oak. Rafe pointed as a tanager flashed through the foliage in a dramatic stroke of red. In the background, the thin whine of cicadas heralded the day's growing heat. Somewhere a hermit thrush trilled its flutelike call.

As Rafe had predicted, there were blackberries. "The ripest ones are hidden on the lower branches, almost touching the ground," he advised as Diana went after them, producing a somewhat crushed paper cup from her pocket that she'd brought for the purpose. "Careful of the brambles. I wouldn't like to see you scratch up that lovely skin."

The intimate quality of his warning caused a tongue of desire to uncurl in some hidden place. The feeling didn't subside though she tried to ignore it as she set to work picking berries. It intensified when, as she emerged from the thicket with a full cup and berry-stained lips, he laughed and opened his mouth.

Diana laughed too. "You look just like a baby bird."

Selecting a plump, reddish-black berry she knew would be particularly sweet, she offered it to him. To her surprise, his lips closed around her fingers. Shivers sped over her skin as he took the berry from between her fingertips with his tongue, then released them slowly with a blunt little kiss.

"Delicious," he murmured.

They started walking again, working their way back toward the head of the canyon. She was only half listening as Rafe told her about the ancient Anasazi who'd once made their homes in the cliffs of white limestone and red rock that overhung the creek bed. Thoughtfully she munched her berries, popping one in his mouth from time to time as if to prove she hadn't been affected all that much by his suggestive behavior.

It was several degrees warmer in the canyon than it had been at his ranch. She pretended not to notice how sexy he looked when he paused to unbutton his shirt as a remedy for the heat.

But the little pantomime they'd enacted had seriously undermined her resolve. It was weakened still further when she almost slipped off one of the round, moss-slickened stones as they forded the tumbling water.

"You'll get your feet wet, *querida*," he said, drawing her firmly against him with one muscled arm.

The soft Spanish endearment went to her head and she let him hold her. "I don't care," she said. "It's so hot I wouldn't mind falling in anyway."

"Well, then, if you're game..."

Disbelief quickened as he bent over to place the canteen and his cigarettes on a flat, dry rock. A moment later she was screaming as he dragged her fully clothed into the icy stream. Wet squished into her boots and soaked through her wool hiking socks. In seconds, her jeans felt like lead from the weight of the water. Her tank top was plastered to her body.

It was scant comfort that Rafe looked even more bedraggled than she felt. "Savage!" she yelled, twisting out of his grasp and splashing him thoroughly in the face.

He grinned, his black hair sticking in damp points to his forehead. "You got that right, Dr. Bailey."

"Oh, but I didn't mean..."

His outrageous grin only broadened. She splashed him again, with mock ferocity this time, aware that he hadn't minded her name-calling at all.

They were both soggy and dripping as they climbed out of the stream on the opposite bank. "At least I'm not hot anymore," Diana said ruefully, wringing out the hems of her form-fitting jeans and sitting down on a broad shelf of rock.

Rafe, who had retrieved his cigarettes and the canteen, slicked his hair back and twisted a bandana around his forehead. The strong Indian look it gave him was startling.

"Savage," she taunted again softly, unable to stop herself.

"What do you expect," he answered, "the way those wet clothes are clinging to your body?"

Suddenly aware of the hard outlines made by her nipples, she didn't reply.

He dropped down beside her, a superbly conditioned male animal who was also a very complex and passionate man. There in the hot sun their garments would dry quickly, even on their bodies. But for the moment, his wet clothes were very revealing too.

Trying not to look at the way they molded to sinew and muscle and bone, or stare at the coppery gleam of his partially bared chest, she sought the imagined safety of his eyes. Promptly she was overcome by the way his long, straight lashes were still damp and sticking together.

"I shouldn't have pushed you into the creek like that, I suppose," he conceded, wiping a berry stain from the corner of her mouth. "I couldn't seem to help it. It's true... you bring out my most uncivilized qualities, just as you make me want to shelter and protect..."

"I didn't mind getting wet," she insisted. "Actually, I liked it."

"So did I."

Seconds passed. She leaned back, looking at him. There was a sense of inevitability as he reached out with one bronze-skinned hand to touch her breast. Lightly he stroked one protruding nipple through the ribbed fabric of her top, causing desire to knife through her with white-hot intensity.

"Rafe..." she whispered.

He transferred his fingers to the closure of her top's placket neckline. "The way you look right now makes me want to touch you all over," he said.

As if in slow motion, her buttons were slipped from their buttonholes. A moment later he was cupping one rose-tipped breast in his warm, callused fingers. "Better than blackberries," he murmured, taking it in his mouth.

Hot currents raged as he sucked at her sensitive bud with sweet, insistent demand. I could die wanting him, she admitted silently, meshing her hands in his hair and supporting his weight as he half covered her with his body.

She would have let him take her there on the red shelf of rock if the sound of whistling and a dog barking as it splashed through the shallows hadn't reached her ears.

"Someone's coming!" she breathed urgently, pushing him off her and covering herself.

Almost simultaneously, the solitary hiker and his dog came into view. "Hello," he waved, not pausing as he went past. His smile told them he knew perfectly well what they had been doing a moment before.

"We can go somewhere else," Rafe suggested quietly when the man had vanished among the trees. "Off the trail, if you want. There are other places."

"No," she said.

Her worries about Josh and what it might mean if she told Rafe yes had returned full-blown. It was easier to hold fast to them now that the passionate momentum of events had faltered.

"Why not?" he asked.

"We just can't. My father..."

He didn't seem to absorb her mention of Josh. Black eyes that had been full of tenderness grew suddenly cold. "Because you're a doctor and I run a helicopter service?" he demanded. "Or does it matter to you that I have relatives on the reservation? Maybe you think you'd find me drunk and freezing some winter night along Santa Fe Avenue?"

"Oh, please!"

There was such genuine distress in her voice that he relented a little. "Look, Diana," he said, "I admit I want to make love to you, and that I'm probably rushing things. But I've wanted you ever since I asked you to dance with me in that bar. I guess I should tell you...sex isn't the only thing I have in mind for us. I'd like the chance to spend time in your company...find out how you think, what makes you smile. And if it matters, I have my doctorate too...in archaeology. I even worked on the Grand Canyon research project for a while..."

Aching that she must refuse him after he'd so humbly laid his accomplishments at her feet, Diana shook her head. "It's not the degree," she told him.

"Then it's the damn Indian thing with you, too. You wouldn't want to bring a man with black hair and high cheekbones home to Daddy."

The words cut deeply as she remembered the smug dinner-table conversation of only a few nights before. "You're only half-right," she said in a strangled voice. "Actually, I *can't* do what you're suggesting...even though I might want to, very much. My father is a narrow-minded old man who doesn't like Indians. I don't happen to agree with him. But he's at risk for another stroke, and I won't do anything to aggravate that."

Rafe was silent for a moment.

"I never thought I'd be saying this," he told her finally, "but he doesn't have to know."

"He *already* knows, don't you see? Reports of what you—what we—were doing outside Doc Furbish's office had reached him by the time I walked in the door."

Tapping out a cigarette, Rafe lit up and blew out a cloud of smoke. "I suppose our trip to the reservation is off, then," he said as if he didn't plan to argue the point.

"On the contrary. A bargain is a bargain."

One dark brow went up at that. "And you're a lady who meets her obligations? Why not just tell me the truth? You want to go out there with me...every bit as much as you wanted what was happening between us a few moments ago."

With effort, she kept her gaze from wavering. "You're right on the money about that," she said. "But I've told you how it has to be."

Neither of them spoke then for a moment.

"I can't understand what your father's problem is," Rafe remarked at last in a softly speculative tone. "Particularly since there's Indian blood in your family too."

Four

At first, his words didn't make any sense. A funny light feeling came over her as she tested them against what she held to be logical and real.

"I don't understand," she said.

Rafe regarded her steadily. "I'm talking about the relatives *you* have on the reservation...on your father's side."

Still she gave him a blank stare.

"I can't believe you don't know about them," he said. "Your mother did. And she was appalled at the way Josh Bailey neglected his own people, wouldn't step in to help when they were in need."

He seemed to be absolutely certain of what he was saying. To Diana, it was as if the world had tilted unexpectedly, or the ground had opened at her feet to reveal a hitherto unknown basis for her life. Absently she did up her buttons. How could Josh have kept such a thing secret all these years? she asked herself. And why does he hate Indians so much if he's one himself?

Then another thought struck her with force. If her father had Indian blood, that made her part Navaho too. If Rafe's story was true, there couldn't be any doubt about the tribe to which her father belonged. With his tall, angular frame and craggy face, his dark, hooded eyes, he was no plump Hopi. He had the Navaho's quick temper and his fierce pride if not his modesty and reserve.

Rafe was watching her quietly. "I'm not saying I believe you," Diana said in answer to his unspoken question. "But I do want to hear more about this . . . anything and everything you can tell."

"All right."

The story that unfolded, there on the rock shelf where they'd almost made love, filled her with amazement.

"As it was told to me," Rafe began, "your great-grandfather, Franklin Parkes, was an army scout in western New Mexico in the 1890s. He fell in love with and married a full-blooded Navaho woman, a skilled weaver and artisan named Annie Little Joe. Eventually he quit his army post to go into ranching, and they came to Arizona, homesteaded a place not far from what was then a much smaller Bailey spread.

"He and Annie had two daughters who took completely opposite paths in life. Laura, the younger, married a Navaho named Joseph Silverhorse and went back to live on the reservation. In just one generation, her children had reduced that branch of the family's Anglo inheritance to one-quarter. Her grandchildren—parallel to you, Diana, on the family tree—are seven-eighths Navaho."

"And the other daughter?" Diana said.

"Her name was Delia."

"My grandmother."

"Yes."

"Tell me . . . please."

"Delia Parkes married Alton Bailey, heir to the neighboring ranch. The two properties were joined shortly afterward when an epidemic claimed her parents. By that time, her only child, Joshua, had already been born."

"Josh doesn't remember his mother very well, just as I don't remember mine," Diana interposed, taking up the story. "I think he was about five when she died, after a fall from a horse. He's always regarded his father's second wife, Jane Tutman Bailey, as the only real mother he ever had."

"Maybe that's more convenient for him, considering how he feels about a large part of his heritage. Naturally, I don't think he had anything to be ashamed of. Have you ever seen a picture of Delia, or of your great-grandmother?"

Diana shook her head. "Not of Annie. If any exist, I don't know about them. I did see a photograph of Delia once. She had dark hair and a long, oval face. But I can't say she looked particularly Indian. Of course, at the time I saw her picture I was just a child. I had no thought of looking for anything like that."

"I don't suppose you did."

A small silence rested between them. Letting Rafe's astonishing revelation sink into her consciousness, Diana didn't feel inclined to challenge it. Though she was carefully reserving judgment with her logical physician's mind, in her innermost heart she was almost ready to believe that what he was saying was the truth.

"The legacy of Annie Little Joe makes your father one-quarter Navaho and you one-eighth," Rafe was saying. "Are you sorry to hear about that, Diana?"

It wasn't hard to guess that he was testing her. Why would I be sorry? she thought. If it's true, then I have that much more right to let you make love to me.

But she knew better than to say such a thing out loud. There were too many questions to ask first, about Josh and the strangers Rafe had said were her Navaho cousins.

"Not sorry," she told him at last. "Just amazed. You have to give me a little time to get used to it."

He nodded, satisfied. "It's common knowledge your mother had a Scandinavian background. And you inherited her gray eyes, blond coloring. But—" he reached out to trace cheekbones that had almost as much height as his "—however faintly, you too carry the look of *Diné*, the People, in your face."

Trying to imagine an Indian background that had remained mostly hidden, yet was part of her genetic structure, intimately interwoven with the very person she was, Diana couldn't find the right words to answer him.

"You have several second and third cousins on the reservation," Rafe added gently, getting to his feet. "I can introduce you to them if you want."

As they rode back up the steeply winding highway to his ranch, Diana's mind was overflowing with a confused jumble of thoughts. Determined to ask her father about what Rafe had told her, she wasn't sure how to approach him. Whatever he said, she'd have to manage it carefully. I'll supplement his answers with my own research if I must, she thought. I won't be put off just because he says it isn't so.

At his corral, Rafe tied up the horses and then turned to face her. "I'm sorry for breaking the news to you about your family so abruptly," he said in a deep, quiet voice. "I can't help but feel I had reasons of my own for doing it, and I hope you'll forgive me for that."

"There's nothing to forgive."

Back in the canyon, the revelation that she and her father might have Indian blood had slowed the tempo of her sexual feelings even as it had claimed all her attention. Now she found herself wishing that Rafe would kiss her again.

Instead, he dug into his jeans pocket and brought forth a peace offering: a little silver ring in the shape of a coyote that weighed lightly in the palm of her hand.

"The coyote is the symbol of my clan," Rafe told her. "I wore this as a child. It should just about fit your finger."

Though she knew very little about Indian lore, Diana remembered hearing somewhere that, in legends, the "coyote people" were Navaho gods. There's no doubt that he's their descendent, she thought; a god in his own right with that beautiful body and fiercely passionate spirit, that innate dignity and gentleness. But I can't take anything of value from him—not yet; and especially not a ring.

He wouldn't let her hand it back to him. "When are we going to tour the reservation together?" he asked instead.

Suddenly she remembered the bargain they'd struck outside Doc Furbish's office and believed she understood his motivation for it. *I imagine he was planning to tell me about Annie Little Joe even then,* she thought. Now she was as eager as he was to make the trip.

"I'm free Wednesday," she said. "Would that be all right?"

Rafe's dark eyes didn't leave hers as he lifted the hand that had closed around his ring to his mouth. "That would be fine with me, Diana," he said.

Back at the Double Bar B, Diana was eager yet reluctant to talk to her father. She found him in his study, going over some books.

"Dad," she said, "I heard quite a story today. I want to know if it's true."

Her use of the name she'd called him as a child gave him some inkling that a serious conversation would be forthcoming. Drawing his brows together, he folded his good hand over the bad one on the desktop and stared at her without reply. She didn't get much of the story out before he was interrupting her to deny vehemently that he had any Indian connections.

"Who the hell put such damnfool notions in your mind, girl?" he demanded, his face ruddy with anger. "That Marquez boy? You been seein' him again?"

Declining to implicate Rafe, Diana named names and outlined the little history she'd heard only that afternoon. Her father's face seemed to crumple. Yet he persisted in his rejection of the tale.

"Got a damn good reason to dislike Indians, and that ain't it," he told her, his speech more slurred than usual as he turned his chair away from her, toward the window. "Told you what it was before. Don't want to talk about it again."

Aching at his displeasure and afraid she'd hurt him deeply, Diana found herself disbelieving him all the same. She was beginning to suspect there was more than just her mother's death in a car crash behind his wall of silence. I'll ask Max, she decided, slipping silently out of the room. Maybe he can he bullied into telling me the truth.

Max Decker was mending a saddle in his combined tack room and office next to the barn. At her questions, his face hardened.

"Don't ask me about that," he thrust back at her, for once forgetting to show any deference. "Go talk to your daddy."

"I have," Diana confessed. "But you know how he is, Max. I don't want to upset him too much."

The implication hung between them that she *would* upset Josh if she must. Max, who had always seemed gruff and not too likable to a small girl growing up on the ranch, was unremittingly loyal to her father.

For a moment, he appeared to struggle with his conscience, but then blurted, "Rafe Marquez told you all this, didn't he?"

Undoubtedly he would report her answer to Josh. She decided it didn't matter; that she had to be frank with him. "Yes," she said.

Max swore. "If you ever tell your daddy I said this, I'll call you a liar," he vowed. "But you're right. He *does* have a better reason than your ma's death in that accident to hate Navahos. I guess you knew she was pregnant at the time she died. Well, the baby she miscarried wasn't his."

Diana stared.

His voice harsh, Max continued, his words sinking into the silence like lead. "She'd been havin' an affair on the reservation, with some young firebrand of a Navaho who kept pushing her to do more and more for his people," he said. "The baby that she bore was dark . . . part-Indian."

Swallowing hard, Diana tried desperately to hang on to reason. "If Josh has Indian blood, that could explain the baby's coloring," she argued.

Her father's foreman uttered another heartfelt oath. "That's crazy and you know it," he said, with so much emphasis she almost believed him.

Agonizing over the conflicting stories she'd heard, Diana stood before her dressing-table mirror that evening in a lace-trimmed shift of transparent cotton, searching her own features as if they were a stranger's.

I do have high cheekbones, she admitted, tracing them with one finger as Rafe had earlier. And is it possible my eyes have a faintly almond shape?

Her short crop of Nordic blond hair and light coloring gave the lie to any notion of Indian kinship. Yet she was one-eighth Navaho, if Rafe was correct.

Cornsilk Woman, she whispered, wondering if the name had always been more appropriate than she'd first guessed. She realized that she *wanted* to be Indian, especially so that her father couldn't view it as betrayal if she let Rafe become her lover.

For that was exactly what she wanted to do. In light of that possibility, she was glad she was so pale. I like the contrast in our coloring, she thought, a little flame of desire licking in her innermost places as she remembered how his thick black hair had felt against her skin, the way the white swell of her breast had looked when captured in his strong brown fingers.

It wasn't hard to imagine how they would appear naked—all ivory and copper, tangled up together in the canyon's underbrush or on her bed's soft sheets.

The image almost too much for her, she shut her eyes and hugged her slim, bare arms. Rafe's silver coyote ring was lying on the dresser where she'd put it that afternoon. Retrieving it, she tried it on the third finger of her left hand.

It was a perfect fit. But there was no way she could wear it in her father's presence—at least not as things stood now. With a sigh, she rummaged in her jewelry case for a sterling chain on which to fasten it. A moment later, she was dropping it beneath her shift, so that it hung like a talisman between her breasts.

I pray Rafe is right and Max is wrong, she thought as she drifted off to sleep. I'm beginning to think I couldn't bear it if my mother had made mistakes that would force me to do without him.

On Wednesday, Diana left for the reservation to meet Rafe. She'd told her father at least a partial truth—that she'd be staying with Buffy in her friend's apartment near the Tuba City health facility. Though he'd grumbled about it, he didn't appear to view the trip as a threat.

Parking the Wagoneer in the dusty parking lot in front of the tiny post office at Gray Mountain Trading Post, she spotted Rafe's truck. Getting out of it, he held open his passenger door.

"Get in quick, Diana," he advised as he took her overnight bag. "There's a dust devil heading this way."

Slamming the door after her, he ran around the truck and got in, barely in time. Seconds later, the dust devil, a relatively harmless miniature whirlwind of sand and grit that would have stung her skin without inflicting serious injury, enveloped them. It whirled about the windows and pinged against the truck's metal surface. Momentarily, it had the effect of isolating them in a cocoon of privacy. In the truck's suddenly cramped space, Rafe's shoulders seemed even broader; his hard, denim-clad thighs felt very near.

If Max is right, am I following in my mother's footsteps? she asked herself. She would have had a reason to feel guilty, and I don't—if I'm willing to ride roughshod over my father's wishes. But her excitement when she met her Indian lover must have been the same as what I'm feeling now.

"Hello," he said, his voice a gentle growl as he put his hand over hers. He made no move to kiss her, except with his eyes.

"Hello," she said.

On the way out to the trading post, she'd considered telling him what Max had said. Now she didn't want to, afraid it would spoil what they could share. The second I'm back in his company, it's just the same, she thought. I want him so much.

"How long can you stay?" he was asking.

"Tonight and tomorrow night. I've arranged to sleep at Buffy's apartment. I'm supposed to see her boss, Dr. Creighton, tomorrow afternoon."

He frowned. "I'm not sure we'll have time to meet your relatives in that case. They live in a remote area across the Utah line. We wouldn't be back until late tomorrow night.''

At his words, Diana was frowning too.

"Never mind, we can come back with the chopper next week," he assured her. "I didn't want us to go that way today, because you'd miss the feel of the land and the way the people live—both are things you can see better from the ground.''

Though she was disappointed, the feeling didn't last. Just being alone with Rafe and exploring the reservation with its vast inhospitable grazing lands and tiny, scattered settlements of hogans would be enough. The delay in meeting her supposed relatives meant she could look forward to a few more days in Rafe's company.

If the desert grasslands of the Bailey winter range, with their scrubby juniper and pinyon seemed barren, then the reservation was like the surface of the moon. Patches of green were rare except for the dusty willows that traced the paths of dry washes, their roots thrust deeply into the dry earth for nourishment. A few sparse herds of sheep grazed in the endless flatlands between the upcropping mesas. But she saw neither shepherds nor Indians on horseback.

On the highway, they passed more pickups, mostly driven by Indians. Usually a man and his wife occupied the trucks' cabs, while several children rode in the flat, open beds. Sometimes a stolid grandmother in an old-fashioned tiered skirt and dark blouse accompanied the little ones, her gray braids protected from the sweeping winds of those open spaces by a scarf.

Diana saw more makeshift roadside stands than houses. Many were abandoned, though a few were attended by one or two brown-skinned women and children who had spread out homemade jewelry for sale.

They stopped at one such stand below the brown hump of a butte. Rafe tipped a boy of about twelve to show them some prehistoric tracks that had been captured eons ago in what had once been the mud of an ancient lake. Now the tracks were fossilized, frozen into the surface of hard red rock, which boasted no soil to soften it, nor grass of any kind. Before they left, Diana bought a seed necklace she didn't particularly want from the boy's smiling mother, who was minding her ten-month-old baby.

By early afternoon they were climbing the steep dirt tracks that led up to the reservation's central mesas to visit the centuries-old dust-colored towns of the Hopi that seemed to cling to thin air and clouds. Everywhere the people were as Buffy had described them that night at the dinner table—intelligent but modest, possessed of an innate dignity and reserve. Amazed at such a different environment so close to the one in which she'd been raised, Diana asked herself over and over if she could claim this as her world too. Even if she couldn't, she was sorry she'd never ventured so far into Indian territory before. Thanks to Josh, she thought, I've missed out on a lot of things.

As the sun started to sink in the west, they were back in Navaho country, far from the place where Rafe said her relatives lived and from Buffy's Tuba City apartment.

"I've arranged for us to stay here with the Yazzie family tonight," Rafe told her, pulling off the winding dirt road by a cluster of hogans. "We'll be back in Tuba City by noon if we get an early start."

He had made his plans without consulting her.
Taken aback, Diana was on the verge of arguing with
him. He might have told me about this when we discussed it before, she thought. But her irritation quickly
gave way to excitement. Except for their Indian hosts,
she would be alone with Rafe in the middle of nowhere. "Won't Buffy worry if I don't show up tonight?" she asked instead.

He shook his head. The protective note in his voice
was very clear. "I told her you'd be with me."

They soon reached the Yazzie home and there Rafe
matter-of-factly introduced her to several rangy, dark-
haired men who were smoking by a cluster of pickup
trucks. He then led her to a small earth and wood hogan that boasted a single door and no windows. "Go
on inside," he told her. "I'll follow in a moment."

Feeling both curious and venturesome, she stepped
into the dim interior. She could see that there was a
smoke hole in the ceiling over what was the fire pit.
Blankets and pots were stored on hooks in the
rounded, shadowed corners of the primitive oval
structure.

She was startled to realize a smiling Indian woman
was offering a basin of fresh water, a cake of soap and
a towel. When Diana accepted it, thanking her, the
woman stated her name, Margaret Yazzie, and bid her
welcome. "Rafe said to give you clean things," she
said, holding out a pile of folded clothing. "If I wash
your jeans and shirt now, they will be dry in the
morning."

Giving herself over to the moment, Diana stepped
out of her dusty garments. Though she'd brought another outfit in her overnight bag, she had no inten-
tion of refusing the woman's friendly gesture. The

proffered clothing turned out to be a wide, tiered Navaho skirt, dark cotton blouse and silver belt. Keeping her back to the door, she washed quickly and then fastened the skirt about her waist.

She was just about to put on the blouse when she heard a footstep behind her. Clutching the garment against her, she whirled about, only to find herself looking into Rafe's black eyes. Surprise and hunger were visible in their depths. Slowly, possessed by some spirit she didn't quite understand, she abandoned her self-protective gesture. Naked to her waist, she stood facing him, her bare nipples hardening in the cool air. The ring he'd given her was cradled in the hollow between her breasts.

Rafe took one step toward her, and then another, his gaze raking like hot coals over her skin. The front of his tight, faded jeans showed his sudden need. Again Diana thought of her willowy blond mother, the smiling woman who'd held her baby self in a dozen family photographs. She imagined Ingrid Bailey standing in a similar hut, about to be undressed completely by the black-haired man she loved.

Then Rafe's hands were covering her, his thumbs pushing at her shadowed buds, and she forgot everything but him. Swaying a little she was overcome by the sharp wave of longing he evoked.

But he wouldn't make love to her, she realized. She could see passion and restraint warring in his face. Restraint was winning, as if he didn't expect her to thank him for overcoming her objections.

Taking the blouse from her hands, he helped her into it, then left it hanging open for a moment. "My little coyote's in a safe place, I see," he said, lifting the ring lightly in his hand. "But you know, don't you, Diana . . . that the ring finger also leads to the heart?"

She didn't have a ready answer and Rafe did up her buttons. Still on fire with wanting him, she let him lead her outside to the largest hogan of the encampment, where the members of the Yazzie family were waiting. The woman who had lent Diana the blouse and skirt motioned her to sit on the floor beside her and her feminine companions. Rafe took his place on the opposite side of the fire pit, with the men.

The Yazzies were serving a typically Navaho mutton stew. Seated there, her blond hair in sharp contrast to the dark heads around her, Diana found the fare greasy, the cornmeal bread that accompanied it tasteless and the coffee bitter. Yet, as her longing for Rafe retreated into some quiet corner, she found herself enjoying the meal, just as she enjoyed the gentle storytelling of a weathered older man and the bright eyes of several children. The children appeared to believe wholeheartedly in the man's tale of how the old gods had brought the first Navahos up from under the earth and given them the land between the four sacred mountains.

As the temperature dropped outside with nightfall, the small fire, for all its smoke, felt more and more like a blessing. It seemed a primitive boon, there in that company that looked much as it might have looked hundreds of years before. Across its leaping flames, she could see Rafe watching her. The gaze that had raked over her earlier with such passion was now full of possessiveness, warm approval and admiration.

"I've always imagined you this way," he told her softly as he led her back to the first hogan when the group separated for the night. "Sitting there with your hair like a yellow flame in the firelight."

"It was a very special time for me," she said.

Not answering, he held a kerosene lantern aloft in the hogan's doorway. Inside, all had been blackness. Now the timbered, sparsely furnished interior of the little dwelling leaped into a chiaroscuro of half-light. The hushed murmur of their hosts' voices seemed suddenly far distant; the wind whistling down off the buttes carried a coyote's howl.

Diana was overcome by a sudden rush of loneliness. "I'm a grown woman," she whispered, "one capable of handling most situations. But I'm ... well, not looking forward to sleeping alone here tonight."

Rafe rested one hand lightly on her shoulder. "I never intended that you should, Cornsilk Woman," he said.

Five

They were standing very close to each other. In that moment, the sexual pull of him was almost too strong to resist. Though Diana hadn't been asking him to make love to her, she was on the verge of letting him do just that—despite the questions about Josh and her alleged Indian heritage that were far from resolved. I probably haven't stopped wanting him since this afternoon, she thought. When his hands covered me like that, I wanted him to go on touching me everywhere.

Now, with the encampment settling down for the night, there would be no one to interrupt them, no one to hear if they cried out softly in the ecstasy of joining their bodies.

"I didn't mean..." she began, looking up at his shadowed face.

Rafe wouldn't let her finish. "I know you didn't," he said. "I plan to sleep beside you, not *with* you, though I'd very much enjoy the latter privilege."

Adjusting the lamp, he hung it from one of the rafters that supported the hogan's low, dome-shaped roof. She could see that someone had brought her duffel bag in from the truck.

"I'll have a cigarette while you change," he was saying. "Call me when you're finished, all right?"

It was clear he didn't plan to take advantage of her, or wrest the decision-making from her hands. Disappointment threatened to engulf desire, and she ached to tell him she hadn't refused him, to confess that she wanted to sleep in his arms. But the reasons to hold back that had reasserted themselves—Josh's hatred of Indians and Max's allegations, even though she didn't quite believe them—made it impossible to find the words.

Keeping his back turned to the hogan's blanket-covered doorway, Rafe stood smoking. Diana, feeling foolish and even childlike, dressed hastily in the thin wisp of a nightgown she'd brought to wear in the guest room of Buffy's warm apartment. Gingerly she slipped beneath the rough, handwoven blanket that covered one of the hut's two cornhusk mattresses. The one on which Rafe would sleep was a few feet away.

When she called out to him, Rafe returned. He stood there looking at her a moment, then said, "Good night, *querida*," And he blew out the lamp so that all was blackness.

"Good night, Rafe," she whispered.

She could hear the soft sounds he made undressing in the dark. Before long, the regular sound of his breathing told her he was asleep.

For her part, Diana lay awake a long time, tossing on the flat, unfamiliar bed. Half-waking thoughts of Josh and the impossible situation his prejudice had produced tormented her mind. At the same time she was tantalized by Rafe's nearness, and the notion that they shared a common heritage—something that should answer Josh's objections.

If Ingrid's baby was dark skinned, as Max claimed, and that Indian strain came from Josh, then I could have a similar baby even if Rafe didn't father it. She briefly wondered how Del would react to that news, but the really stunning idea didn't involve Del at all. She was overwhelmed at the thought of herself and the half-Indian pilot making a child together.

Stop it! she demanded of herself in no uncertain terms. You know that even if we are part Navaho, Josh would never admit it. If you married someone like Rafe, he'd never speak to you again.

It occurred to her that she had long since stopped thinking strictly in terms of a brief fling where the man sleeping a few feet away from her was concerned. In truth, thanks to her emotional involvement with him, she'd almost forgotten her fellowship back east— something she'd felt extraordinarily lucky to win before coming back to Arizona and seeing Rafe.

Even if there weren't far more serious problems, learning to care deeply for Rafe could upset all your plans, she warned herself. You'd be wise to back away. Maybe so, came the answer from her heart. But isn't it already too late?

At last she fell into a fitful slumber, only to awaken at about 3:00 a.m. to bone-penetrating cold. For some time she lay still, huddled in a ball and trying to endure the chill, not knowing where to find another blanket in the dark.

Finally, too frozen to go back to sleep, she whispered Rafe's name in desperation. Instantly he was awake, like some wild animal that remains watchful even as it sleeps.

"What is it, Diana?" he said softly.

"I'm freezing." She realized she sounded like a petulant child. "Could you possibly...move over a little closer and share your blanket?"

His response was a wry chuckle. "I'm not wearing anything. You'll have to wait a moment while I put on my jeans."

Rafe had been lying there naked beneath his blanket only a few feet away. She shivered a little, partly from the cold and partly from imagining how he must look, pulling on his jeans in the dark.

His zipper rasped shut and then she heard the snap on his waistband closing. He didn't need to light the lantern or grope about to find her. Unerringly, though she didn't speak to guide him, he dragged his corn-husk mattress beside hers.

"You'll have to spread out your blanket so that it can cover both of us," he directed.

Uncurling, she did as he asked, then felt the weight of his blanket being added to hers. A moment later, he had crawled beneath both blankets and drawn her into his arms. Though she knew he would be aware of her body's every curve and hollow through the thin nightgown, she didn't feel awkward or shy. Instead, she had the profoundly safe feeling of coming home to a haven that had always been hers to claim.

He wasn't wearing a shirt. She cuddled close to the hard warmth of his chest, another wave of gooseflesh passing over her skin, and put her arms around him.

His deep voice was full of concern. "Diana...you really are cold, sweetheart."

"I'll be fine now," she said.

"Sure?" He chafed her arms.

She nodded, able to feel the steady beating of his heart. Already her chill was subsiding as she inhaled his scent and felt his warm breath on her forehead. His muscled thighs pressed firmly against her own.

I'm mad for him, she thought. All caution be damned. The hard, lean length of him, those beautifully shaped hands that could give me such pleasure. His wry humor, the deep wellspring of his passion, the essential person that is Rafe Marquez, are what I want.

Yet incredibly, she also wanted to sleep. She could feel her eyelids growing heavy and rational thought slipping from her grasp as she burrowed deeper against him. Despite all efforts to stay awake and experience every nuance of what was happening between them, she was soon lost in dreams. This time it was he who lay awake, staring at the dark.

In the morning, she opened her eyes to find him gone. Then she heard his voice outside the hogan, mingled with that of another man, and knew he'd risen early to avoid awkward complications. I wouldn't have looked at it like that, she thought. I *wanted* to wake up in his arms.

Dressing in the now clean jeans and shirt that had been left beside her bed, Diana went out into the sunlight. Immediately Rafe paused in his conversation with the old man who had told stories around the fire the night before. She thought she could see in his eyes a glimmer of the deprivation she felt. But he didn't allude to it in company, and only asked her how she'd slept.

"Wonderfully," she answered, causing a little muscle to quirk in his jaw. "I can't remember when I've been so comfortable."

Slowly Rafe shook his head. "I don't know if *comfortable* is exactly the word I'd choose, Diana," he said.

After sharing a simple breakfast with their hosts, they got into the truck for the ride back to Tuba City. Waving goodbye to the smiling woman who'd washed her clothes, Diana decided to take hold of the situation. "I'm curious about something," she told him as they drove away. "To be blunt, I'm wondering why you didn't take advantage of what happened last night."

His swift glance was so full of feeling it nearly took her breath away. "Let me assure you, Diana," he said with sober directness, "it wasn't for lack of desire. It's just that I've decided you'll want me as much as I want you when finally we come together... so much that your father and our different worlds won't matter. I'm going to let you pick the right time and place for us, sweetheart."

There was nothing she could say to that, and they fell into an emotionally charged silence. Unfair tactics, Diana complained to herself. But she had to admit the truth. Somehow he'd realized what was only now fully apparent to her: She'd wanted him to overcome her objections so that she wouldn't be responsible for going against her father.

Unlike Del and some other men she'd known, he was too wise and self-contained for that. Instead, he respected her as a person, as a grown woman who could make her own choices and take the consequences. He'd made it clear, too, that what he wanted went far beyond an opportunity to lose himself in the pleasures of her body. Instead, it had more to do with her abandoning her defenses and becoming totally his.

He didn't seem to doubt that it would happen. After all, he'd said *when*, not *if* when he'd spoken of them coming together. I hope he's right, Diana thought. I'll always regret it if I don't taste his love.

It seemed only minutes until they were entering the outskirts of Tuba City, with its ubiquitous pickup trucks, fried-chicken palaces and red sandstone government buildings. She spotted several young Indian men with Rafe's rangy build and dark hair, striding along in T-shirts and jeans. For the most part, their coloring was darker than his and their faces were broader, their eyes more almond-shaped. Observing them, she found it easier to pick out the traits of Rafe's Spanish heritage.

The U.S. Public Health Service hospital where Buffy worked was a low, tan brick building next to the tiny Tuba City airport. It faced a trailer park. Beyond the trailers were the brown frame apartments where Buffy had been renting a place.

Rafe went into the hospital with her, saying he had also very much wanted her to meet Dr. Creighton. They found Buffy and her boss in the children's clinic, administering polio vaccinations. The youngsters, dusky skinned and wide-eyed at the sight of the vaccination needle but bravely enduring it, charmed

Diana on the spot. My little brother would have looked like them if he'd lived, she realized.

Without a break in her brisk, professional manner, Buffy searched Diana's face and then glanced at Rafe. Probably the sparks between us are too obvious to miss, Diana thought. I wonder what she'd say if she knew we'd slept together?

Quickly it became clear that, while Buffy simply wanted Diana to meet her boss as a medical colleague, Rafe had something more in mind. It didn't take him long to elicit for her benefit that Dr. Creighton would be flying home to Oregon that weekend on family business.

"I might be gone for as long as a month," Larry Creighton said with a frown, his busy hands examining a child's chest and stomach for abnormalities. "Meanwhile, this clinic is going to suffer. We're shorthanded already, as Buffy can attest. The new outreach program, which takes advantage of Rafe's helicopter service, is going to go by the boards altogether, I'm afraid."

Looking at the children who were lined up for their shots, Diana wished there was something she could do.

"I'd like to help for as long as I'm in the area," she said. "Unfortunately, I'm licensed in Maryland, not Arizona."

Larry Creighton regarded her thoughtfully. "If you mean that," he said, "licensure shouldn't be a problem. Both this facility and the reservation are under federal jurisdiction. Your Maryland license should be acceptable."

Diana hesitated. She knew Josh would be furious if she followed in her mother's footsteps and helped the Indians. But if we have relatives out here, relatives we've neglected all these years, she thought, helping with the clinic and the outreach program would be a way of making up for that. It might even give me a chance to get to know my Indian cousins.

She could feel Rafe looking at her, waiting to see how she would resolve the situation. "In that case, since my father is progressing nicely, I can afford to give you several days a week until mid-September," she told Larry Creighton. "I'm due back at Johns Hopkins to take up a fellowship then."

Rafe's dark brows knitted together at her words. Though he plainly approved of her decision to help the clinic, he wasn't pleased to be reminded, she guessed, that her sojourn in Flagstaff was only a temporary one. Buffy and Larry Creighton, however, showed their unmitigated delight.

The tall blond doctor clapped her on the arm with gratitude. "You don't know what this means to me," he said. "If you can cover until then, I might be able to find someone for the week or two after you're gone. Of course, we've arranged for a nurse to take Buffy's place when she's on her honeymoon."

Between them, they arranged that Diana would spend that afternoon and the following day at the clinic, learning its procedures and catching up on the outreach program. For the moment, it seemed, the remainder of her reservation tour with Rafe had been indefinitely postponed.

He seemed to realize it too. "You'll have a chance to meet the people we were talking about next week," he told her quietly. "We have an outreach day planned at Magic Butte."

"That's good." Already she'd picked up a stethoscope.

"I half expected Rafe to join us this evening," Buffy said at the end of the day as they walked past the trailer park toward her apartment.

Diana was noncommittal. "He had some business to attend to, as long as I'd be staying with you."

"Speaking of that, where *did* you stay last night?"

"With some Indian friends of his. In a hogan. We slept on the ground."

Buffy gave her a look. "Not very communicative about it, are you? What's going on, anyway? Are the two of you having an affair?"

"I don't know what you mean."

But Buffy was not the sort to let her off the hook so readily. "Don't kid your pal," she chided. "I saw the way he looked at you. And the way you seem to avoid looking at him, at least for public consumption. What gives?"

They were at the door of Buffy's apartment, and Diana had half a moment's grace while her friend inserted the key and led the way into a cozy living room she had decorated with knickknacks, secondhand overstuffed furniture and gingham pillows.

"Well?" Buffy asked, flopping down on the couch and unlacing her white nurse's oxfords. "Are you sleeping with Rafe? Because if it's true, you're crazy to be staying here with me tonight."

On the opposite end of the couch, Diana kicked off her own suede loafers and drew up her knees, hugging them with her arms. "The answer to your question is both yes and no," she said.

Buffy's eyebrows soared. "Care to explain?"

Slightly embarrassed, Diana complied. As she did so, she was lost in remembering what it was like to sleep sheltered in Rafe's arms.

"I can't pretend I don't want him," she confessed, meeting her friend's sympathetic gaze. "But there's so much standing in the way...Josh, my fellowship and something else I can't even tell you about yet. I guess last night I was hoping he would take the decision-making out of my hands. But he didn't, because he wants it to be my choice as much as his. My rational side keeps telling me it would be a disaster to get involved with him."

Shaking her head, Buffy got up to pop two TV dinners into the oven. "Better get your disaster plan ready then," she advised. "Because I think you're going to need it."

In the morning, Diana reported at the clinic again. She worked a full schedule that day, seeing patients for Larry Creighton so that he would have time to confer with her late that afternoon about what needed to be done in his absence. It seemed he'd had no trouble at all getting permission from the health facility director for her to fill in for him.

Rafe didn't put in an appearance until about 5:00 p.m., after the last of their patients had gone out the door. "Got your things together?" he asked. "Or do we have to go by Buffy's and get them first?"

For a moment she wasn't quite sure what to say to him. He expected to drive her back to Gray Mountain, that much was certain. And she wanted to go with him. But she'd told him she was free for only two nights for a reason. She'd promised to attend a Friday-night cookout with Rob, Buffy and Del at Rob's town home near the Fairfield Country Club.

"Buffy's driving me," she said at last, unbuttoning her borrowed lab coat and removing the stethoscope from around her neck. "I wasn't sure you were coming back. It's all arranged."

"I thought we could have dinner together this evening, if you don't have other plans," he insisted quietly, his black eyes intense.

"I'm sorry. I really do have an engagement."

Perversely, then, she told him about the cookout at Rob's place, and the fact that Del would be there.

Rafe gave her a little grimace. "I don't suppose mutton will be on the menu."

"No...I don't suppose."

There was a small silence between them. "Is Del trying to revive your old romance?" he asked.

Nothing had happened yet between them to give him the right to ask her such a personal question. Yet she felt compelled to answer it. "Probably," she said. "And I do like him, very much. But friendship with Del is where I intend to draw the line."

"That's good." Lightly he placed one hand on her arm and she felt herself go weak at the sexual magnetism of him. "I meant what I said yesterday morning, Diana," he said, "about letting you choose the time and place for us. If you get bored with your barbecue this evening, you know where to find me."

The cookout on Rob's brick patio, with its view of the smoky-blue San Francisco peaks, was pleasant but a little tedious after her adventure on the reservation. Sitting back in one of the lattice chairs with a margarita in her hand, Diana smiled coolly in her slim, cream-colored silk broadcloth dress and let the casual conversation flow around her.

As she'd expected, Del pulled his chair up beside hers and made a series of possessive gestures that she unobtrusively and gently repulsed. But her attention was only half concentrated on keeping him at bay. Again and again she returned to the remembered sensation of Rafe's body pressed against hers under the rough blanket, to his words as they had parted that afternoon.

Maybe he's right and it's inevitable that we should become lovers, she thought, stunned at the rush of feeling that overwhelmed her when she contemplated just letting go and following her heart. Maybe it was ordained by the old Indian gods from the moment we met so many years ago.

There were powerful reasons to go against fate—not the least of which involved her mother's supposed affair. But if she didn't accept what the gods were offering, she thought, then she'd deserve to regret it with all her heart.

After supper, they danced a little on the patio. Buffy and Rob, whose wedding was less than two weeks away, were wrapped tightly together. In Del's arms, Diana was merely going through the motions. By the time the party broke up, she had made her choice.

"I really think I should go straight home tonight," she told Del when he asked her to join him for a nightcap at the house he'd recently purchased nearby. "I practiced a full day of medicine, you know. I could use the rest."

"I understand." Disappointment written all over his face, Del gave her a deferential good-night kiss.

She let him back out of Rob's driveway first, though he couldn't have guessed what was on her mind. And she did go straight home to the house on Mount Pleasant Road just as she'd said—long enough to throw some underwear and a few essential toiletries into her most capacious leather purse.

Josh, many miles distant at the winter headquarters of the Bailey spread, would never know. She hung back a moment before the bedroom's oval pier glass, caught by her own wild gray-eyed glitter of anticipation. Maybe this is wrong, she thought defiantly. But I want him—enough to risk everything just to know his love.

Driving down 89A in the velvety late-summer night, she felt a little shaken by what she was about to do. But that didn't dissuade her from her purpose. It wasn't long before she'd reached the open gate to Rafe's property and turned onto the gravel drive that led to his house.

It was a dark night, but cool and clear; the sky was full of stars. As she approached the house, she could see that smoke was rising from one of the octagonal cedar house's stone chimneys. A few lights were burning. Rafe's truck was in the drive and the helicopter was resting on its landing pad by a small corrugated metal hangar.

From the barn she could hear the soft blowing of one of the horses. But there was no sign of Rafe's hired man about the place.

Her heart beating faster, Diana shut off the Wagoneer's engine and got out, quietly shutting the door. She wasn't exactly sure where the house's front entrance was. Feeling light-headed and a little shocked at herself, she stepped up onto his cedar deck and randomly slid one of the glass patio doors ajar.

The room she'd chosen to enter was the place where he slept. For a moment she hesitated but then stepped inside, looking about her. Priceless Navaho rugs, in soft earthen tones and ochers and crimsons, hung from cedar and stone walls, met her eye. A huge rough-hewn bed was covered with a sheepskin throw. As she'd expected, there was an expanse of skylight. From the big stone hearth, the fire she'd noted from outside cast a rose-colored glow.

"Is that you, Diana?" Rafe's voice, deep and a little rough, came from behind her.

She turned to face him. He was standing in the open doorway to his sauna. Gleaming with sweat, his body was wrapped sarong-style in a thick white towel that set off his bronze coloring. In that moment, Diana was certain there wasn't a more magnificent man in all creation.

"The sweat bath is a venerable Indian cure for what ails you," he remarked softly when she didn't speak.

"What ails you?" she repeated after him, putting it like a question.

"You." His black eyes seemed to look into her very soul.

"I choose here and now," she told him, taking a step in his direction. "Because you ail *me*, Coyote Man. You ail me, too."

Six

His towel dropped to the floor as he enfolded her so fiercely she thought her bones would break. She could feel his hard nakedness as he buried his face in her neck. For the first time she realized fully how Rafe's desire for her must have smoldered for years, to blaze up when they met again at the Weatherford and consume her too. If she did have Indian blood, it was on fire now, aching to mate with his.

He didn't say a word. Instead he devoured her with blunt little kisses that pressed against her eyelids, her cheeks, her mouth. A moment later, his tongue was parting her lips, probing sweetly as if to offer a foretaste of his love. Mindless, she gave herself over into his keeping. All the barriers that had seemed so forbidding were crashing at their feet.

Eyes shut, Diana tilted her lower body against him. The firm outline of his passion made her feminine emptiness want to open for him like a well. Her nipples were hardening into tight buds and she could feel the warmth of her own need flooding through her body.

"Rafe, I want you so much," she begged.

"My sweet Diana." Muffled against her, the words seemed to catch in his throat.

She was still fully clothed, and he relaxed his hold on her a little, running his hands over her soft curves through the sleek, sensuous fabric of her dress. But the intensity of his embrace didn't lessen for that. One hand took possession of her buttocks to draw her closer still, molding her to even more intimate knowledge of his arousal.

"You have such a gorgeous body," he whispered.

She shook her head. You're the beautiful one, she told him silently, free at last to explore his hard curves and angles, to learn the man-scented texture of his skin.

With a deference that was almost old-fashioned, he reached for her buttons. She didn't doubt it was mixed with lust. His dark eyes blazing, he opened the front of her dress and slipped it slowly from her shoulders. It slithered down over her hips and fell to her ankles in a silken heap.

Her thin wisp of a bra came next, unclasping at the hollow where his ring nestled, to spill her breasts into his hands. Clutching at his corded biceps, she swayed a little at what he was making her feel.

"Silk and velvet," Rafe murmured, his proud warchief/conquistador's features blurring with passion. "You have the most beautiful breasts in the world." If she thought she'd known need before, Diana learned she was mistaken. Not even the passion they'd

shared in the sunlit canyon could compare with what
she experienced in that moment. Sharp stabs of longing pierced her to the quick as he sucked at one nipple, gently mauling it as if he would draw all the
sweetness from her body. She shuddered with delight
as strong brown fingers took hold of her other breast
to massage its rosy bud between their tips.

The exquisite messages that were telegraphed from
her delicate peaks to the place where she needed him
most wouldn't let her wait. Tangling her fingers in his
hair, she pleaded with him.

"I want you... Please, darling...let me take off the
rest of my things."

He was licking at her now, first one breast and then
the other, making her half wild with longing. "If that
would please you," he answered. "I want to kiss you
all over, white doe of my love."

She was wearing very little, after all, just a transparent bikini and lace-trimmed garter belt, her heels
and sheer, off-white stockings. Her breasts damp from
his mouth, Diana stepped out of her beige sandals and
kicked them aside. Still half kneeling before her, Rafe
took off her stockings while she balanced with her
hands on his shoulders. Then he unfastened the garter
belt and slid the tiny diaphanous bikini from her hips.

Her breath was coming in ragged gasps when finally he released her. "Rafe . . . for God's sake, I need
you."

"You'll have me," he promised. "And all the pleasure and adoration I can give. But not so quickly, not
yet. Even though it's the first time, I want to make it
last."

Sheltering her with one arm, he drew her toward the
sauna's open door. Inside the light was dim, fogged by

steam from the hot pit of stones. The heat hit her in a wave and she took a deep breath to accommodate it.

Gently Rafe turned her around to face him. They stood embracing lightly on the wooden platform that surrounded the fire pit.

"Tradition says lightning will strike us...an unmarried man and woman going into the sweat bath together," he warned, his tongue lightly nuzzling at her mouth. "But then it's going to strike anyway, isn't it?"

"Let it," she replied. "If we have to take it slow, then I want to make you crazy too."

On one side of the low pit of stones were a tatami mat and some handwoven pillows. They sank down together, wrapped in each other's arms. Knowing he was hers now and throttling her urgency, Diana began to caress him as he'd caressed her, biting lovingly at his flat male nipples and tracing the line of crisp dark hair that grew to his navel.

"Your Spanish heritage," she whispered. "Indians have smooth bodies."

"Like yours, Diana."

"Yes, I want to be Indian for you, Rafael," she said. Daring to caress him as she had in her imagination.

"Touch me, I want you to," he urged, his voice ragged with emotion. In the next breath he was forcing her to stop, clearly struggling with a control he had almost lost.

"Let me have you," she insisted, moving up to kiss his mouth.

This time, he gave way to her demands. But he didn't move to lie atop her in the conventional way of making love. Sweating profusely, his coppery skin gleaming so that every muscle and contrasting hollow was defined, Rafe sat cross-legged on the mat-covered platform.

"Now...cover me," he asked, inviting her to straddle him.

She gave a wordless cry as she lowered herself for him to enter, felt him claim the empty place that had always been his. With Rafe inside her, time and space seemed to fall away. She entered a separate world where only he and she existed, shutting out everything but the steamy cocoon of the cedar-walled room and the miracle of the two of them joined together.

Lovingly he kissed her mouth. "Sit all the way down on my lap, darling," he coaxed tenderly. "Wrap your legs around me and hold me close."

Tingling all over, she did as he suggested. From the blind look on his face, she knew he was once again fighting to maintain control. He had all of her now, just as she had him. But she was greedy to feel him moving inside her; with all her being, she wanted to pull him deeper still. Instinctively she tightened her hold and Rafe thrust upward to accommodate her, then was motionless. The hot, diffuse glow kindled by his presence spread like wildfire through her body.

They sat that way for some moments, moving only a little as their longing crested in waves, murmuring endearments and caressing each other face-to-face. The heat of the sauna that made her body glisten like polished ivory was nothing compared to the conflagration within.

"I always dreamed this moment would come for us," Rafe told her, his eyes so full of lust and adoration she could have wept.

"Yes, oh, yes, Coyote Man..."

In her heart, she went on to tell him the complete truth: I've always known it was you I loved.

Prodded perhaps by a confession he could only sense, he began to move—slowly at first, and then with mounting urgency. Diana responded with an answering rhythm of tightening and release that was as old as time and as instinctive as her womanly self.

In that juxtaposition, his pressure against her most responsive feminine places seemed too exquisite to bear. If we go any higher, I won't be able to stop myself, she thought, only dimly realizing how her inner thighs had tensed and her whole body gone rigid as it reached for consummation.

But by then, it wasn't possible to retreat. The floodgates opened and she broke free in spasms of delight, bending like a bowstring and crying out his name. Her incandescence ignited his, and he followed within seconds. Shivers passed fiercely over his skin as he shook with the tremors of his own fulfillment, his cries at least as helpless as hers.

Gradually they quieted. All her makeup was gone and her hair was damply clinging to her forehead. Yet she felt beautiful, powerful, part of the earth. A pleasant ache of satisfaction had settled in her thighs and she was still floating on the feeling of what they had shared, tingling with it, to the very soles of her feet.

"'In beauty it is finished,'" Rafe whispered, cradling her face in his hands.

She recognized the traditional ending to every Navaho prayer. I've never been so happy, she thought. In the same moment, she realized she was a little dizzy, too, almost prostrated by the heat.

Immediately he caught it. "Darling," he said with swift remorse, "you're not used to the sauna like I am. I have to get you out of here, cool off your skin."

She didn't want to venture from his embrace, except perhaps to lie down on the tatami mat with her head pillowed against his shoulder. Somehow he persuaded her to her feet.

"This will be better," he said, leading the way into his adjoining bath. "A shower first, to rinse off our sweat. I'll rub you dry and then cuddle you under the blanket."

She stood passive under the spray as he soaped her body and washed her short blond curls. How handsome he is with his hair shiny-wet and plastered to his head, she thought. My lover. Satisfaction deepened inside her like a slow, pervasive tide.

They rinsed, and the cool stream of water felt like ice on her heated skin. But she was soon dry, chafed by a thick towel in Rafe's hands.

For a moment, he paused and nuzzled her neck with kisses. "Your skin smells so sweet, I can't get enough of it," he said, the crease beside his mouth deepening. "If you stay and sleep with me tonight, I can't promise I won't want you again."

"I wouldn't let you promise that." Reawakened by the cool water, she reached up to touch that little quirking line as she'd imagined herself doing so many times. "By the way, I didn't bring a nightgown. I hope you don't plan to wear your jeans."

The night had turned very cool, as even late-August nights could do at that altitude. As they returned to the bedroom, she saw that the fire had died down to embers. Folding the sheepskin throw back to the foot of his big bed, Rafe turned down the blanket. Diana stretched out on the smooth sheet, her clean hair fluffed out like a halo on his pillow.

"You're so lovely," he said, looking at her.

She held out her arms.

In the room's soft glow, it was possible to see their reflections in the skylight overhead. Dimly she could make out the contrast between their bodies. Rafe didn't speak but she knew what he was thinking.

"I like the different colors we are," she told him, stroking his chest and flat, hard stomach. "I think we're beautiful together."

In response, he pulled up the blanket and switched off the lamps. Above them, the billion stars that littered the Arizona night sky sprang forth in all their brilliance. For several minutes they just lay there looking at them, with their arms about each other.

"Diana?" Rafe asked finally, his voice deep and a little rough beside her ear.

"Yes, darling?"

He didn't answer.

"Come here," she said, understanding him perfectly. "I'm not ready to go to sleep either."

With a little groan she knew was an endearment, he moved back between her legs.

Rain was pattering against the glass bubble overhead and a gray, soft light filled the room when she awoke. At first, Diana didn't quite open her eyes. Content to drift in the memory of what had happened between them, she wove her first waking thoughts about the words he'd spoken after their second lovemaking. "Sleep now, Cornsilk Woman," he'd whispered, "safe in the knowledge you've given me more pleasure than I've ever known."

Then she missed the hard bulk of his body against hers and reached for him only to find him gone. But he hadn't wandered far; a moment later he walked in, comfortably naked still, carrying coffee on a tray.

She sat up, not minding that the sheet didn't cover her.

"Good morning," she said, smiling as he put down the tray on top of the bedclothes and leaned over to kiss her mouth.

"The very best."

He sat down beside her, pouring out her coffee and handing her the cup. "I'll cook if you're hungry," he offered. "Anything you want, just to keep you in my house."

But she couldn't stay for long. Josh would be calling her at their place in town, and would worry if she were absent for any length of time. Sipping the steaming brew, she let her eyes linger on the bronzed torso she had kissed, then lifted them to explore the planes and angles of his face.

How I want him, despite the forces at work to separate us! she thought, setting her cup aside on the night table and coming back into his arms. "Make love to me slowly this time," she begged. "When we finish, I have to go."

Much later, when she had dried off from another shower and was hunting up her clothes, Rafe asked her how soon they would be seeing each other again.

"I have to spend some time with my father this weekend, particularly since I'll be out on the reservation several days next week," she reminded him.

With obvious regret, he admitted that he understood. "Are you going to tell him about us?" he asked.

"I can't . . . not yet."

Rafe was silent a moment. "We're scheduled for T.B. screenings and general health exams by chopper up near the Utah border on Tuesday," he said finally. "Where do you want me to pick you up?"

Diana slipped her arms about his neck as if in apology. "We can meet at the landing strip next to the hospital," she said.

Driving back to the house on Mount Pleasant Road so that she could change before putting in an appearance at the ranch, Diana faced the enormity of what had happened. The fact that she and Rafe were lovers would seem bad enough if Josh found out. But that wasn't the worst of it, by a long shot. We weren't just having sex there in Rafe's sauna or in his bed, she admitted to herself. What we were making was *love*, even though neither of us spoke the word.

Love meant something more than a secret fling kept quiet so it didn't hurt anyone and then abandoned when she left Flagstaff to resume her regular life. Whether she were to marry Rafe someday and have his children or just carelessly let the news of their affair leak out because she was drawn to take greater and greater risks, it would kill Josh—particularly if Max's terrible story was true.

In her mind's eye she pictured the unthinkable scenario of bringing Rafe home for a dinner like the one where she'd been paired with Del. In the unlikely event that her father would allow it at all he'd be privately devastated. Seeing her tall, part-Navaho man beside her would only remind him of his life's greatest sorrow.

I don't know where we can go from here, she sighed, letting herself into the house and changing into her jeans. Giving up Rafe is out of the question now. And I don't want to lose my father or break his heart.

This time, Josh didn't have even an inkling about where she'd been. Arriving at the ranch, she found him sitting in his wheelchair under a spreading sycamore tree with the newspaper in his lap.

"Del said you were tired from gallivantin' around after those Indians with Buffy," he said, putting the paper aside. "I would've called and invited you to breakfast, but I thought you might want to get your beauty sleep."

Oops, thought Diana. Already he and Del have been on the phone. "I really appreciate that, Josh," she teased lightly. "Now that I'm pushing thirty, I have to get all the beauty sleep I can."

"Hell, you're the prettiest daughter a man could want."

Automatically Diana bent to take his pulse. There in the desert it hadn't rained, and she wasn't sure he should be out in the heat. His pulse was normal, though, if faintly erratic.

"It's getting hot out here," she told him. "Don't you think I should take you back in the house?"

"An old desert rat like me? Huh." Josh gave her one of his wily looks. "That boy, Del...you know he's stuck on you, sugar."

Diana didn't answer, bracing herself for the sales pitch she was about to get.

"Make you a damn good husband if you were to change your mind and settle here," he added.

In his eyes, she knew, that was the truth. She wasn't sure how to take exception to it without running down Del. "You know I plan to start my fellowship in a couple of weeks," she compromised, realizing in the same breath how tentative those plans had become.

For a while neither of them said anything more as they gazed quietly out at the vast panorama of ranch country that had met their eyes for years. I think I'll go riding this afternoon, Diana decided. I have a lot to think about.

Apparently Josh had been thinking too. "Don't like it much, the way you've been hangin' around with Indians," he said.

Diana gave him a swift, appraising look. "Because my mother worked out there, and you didn't approve of it?" she asked.

She didn't mention Ingrid's accident, though she knew it must be on his mind. Instead, she was holding her breath against the possibility he'd tell her the story Max had told and get it out in the open between them.

But maybe there's no such story to tell, she reminded herself, clinging to her skepticism as if it were a life raft.

"That's part of it," Josh said at last.

"Dad..." She hesitated, then decided her reasons were good enough to forge ahead. "Please don't be angry with me. But I have to know...could there possibly be even a little Indian blood in our family line?"

"No way in hell!" Her father's eyes blazed and he clenched his good fist, a sure sign of fury. "It's that Marquez boy who put you up to this," he accused harshly. "I hope to God you're not seeing him, girl."

At least he hadn't called Rafe a bastard this time. But she still wasn't ready to discuss a relationship that had changed overnight into the most important thing in her life.

"There must be records," she said. "If you won't talk about this, I'll find out on my own at the courthouse."

Josh's face darkened, and she was assailed by the sudden fear that she'd gone too far. Then he settled back in his chair, forcing himself into some semblance of complacency. "Nothin' there for you to find," he said.

The subject was closed—permanently, she guessed—unless she did the unthinkable and laid Max's story beside him. I really might end up taking him to the hospital if I did that, she admitted to herself.

"I don't understand why you must hate a whole culture because of what one person did," she said, pushing things as far as she dared.

Her father didn't answer, and she was left to wonder if he was hiding the truth about his Indian blood or Ingrid's affair...or perhaps some even darker secret she knew nothing about.

That afternoon, she rode out a seeker in the high desert chaparral, tracing the maze of tracks left by tires and hoofprints as her father's wranglers moved through the brush checking on cattle. But the endless rises dotted with juniper and pinyon trees, the blue peaks in the distance, had no easy answers.

Seven

On Tuesday at Tuba City, Diana and Buffy grabbed up their screening supplies and ran out to the helipad where Rafe was just setting down. It was the first time Diana had seen him in the helicopter, and she watched him land with fascination, squinting from behind dark glasses to protect her eyes from the maelstrom of dust.

To Buffy's surprise, he took off his headphones and got out to enfold Diana in his arms. "Hello, darling," he whispered, kissing her fully on the mouth.

"Rafe," she said.

She couldn't deny she was keenly aware of her friend's astonishment and interest, but any slight embarrassment she might have felt was overcome just by holding his tall body in her arms. Even there, in the hard-edged morning light, whipped by the wind from his slackening propellers, she could feel their intimacy like a glowing coal.

"I love you," he said, low enough that Buffy couldn't hear it, and then added, "I have to go in the hospital to make a phone call. It'll only take a minute or so."

"Disaster struck already, huh?" Buffy climbed into the back seat and piled the screening things beside her so that Diana could sit in the front with Rafe.

Diana kept her voice as noncommittal as possible. "I guess you could say so."

"You don't seem all that thrilled about it."

She twisted in her seat, meeting her friend's curious blue gaze. "That's where you're wrong," she admitted. "I feel so much that it frightens me."

"Ohh." Buffy nodded as if satisfied. "I think I was hoping this would happen," she said. "Partly for selfish reasons, because I miss you and wish you'd come back here to live. And partly because I think the world of Rafe Marquez. You know I love Rob, and he doesn't enter into this. But I've always thought Rafe was the only man I knew who was special enough to satisfy you."

Diana gave her a wry grin. "He does that, all right."

"Good." Her friend's open, freckled face creased in an approving smile. "You need to be a woman too, Diana, not just a doctor."

"Well, of course I do. It doesn't bother you . . . that he's part Indian?"

"Not particularly. Does it bother you?"

Quite the opposite, Diana realized. "Actually, I think that's one of the things I like most about him," she said. "I know that sounds terrible. And the truth is, I'd be wild about him in any case. But there's more to it than just his being part Indian, Buf . . . Rafe tells me Josh and I have Navaho blood too."

Buffy's eyes flew open. "You're kidding! How can that be, the way your father feels?"

Diana's attention shifted to the window. Rafe was striding back toward the chopper, his black hair attractively disarranged by the wind. He was wearing what were probably his oldest jeans; faded and threadbare, they fit his long thighs and hard, slim legs like a glove, reminding her of all the pleasure his wonderful body could give. He's a man in a million, she thought. And he's mine if I have the courage to go against my father's wishes.

There on the runway he'd told her that he loved her, and she knew it was the simple truth. Though she'd longed to say she felt the same about him there hadn't been time, any more than there was time now to elaborate for Buffy on her alleged Indian heritage.

She turned to face the instrument panel again as he walked around the chopper to the pilot's side.

"Whether you're Navaho or not, Rafe Marquez is perfect for you," her friend pronounced in her ear. "I hope you have enough sense not to make any dumb sacrifices."

Then the man she loved was settling in the cockpit and giving her a brilliant smile. He revved up his craft's engines so that the rotor blades turned faster and faster, finally giving off the characteristic chopping sound. They lifted off, tilting away at an angle from the airfield and the hospital, rising as if they were in an elevator over the sycamore trees and red stone government buildings. Beneath them the flat and uninspired terrain of Tuba City spread out, its highest point the municipal water tower. They were heading northeast, toward the distant buttes.

The roar of the engines was deafening and Rafe handed her a pair of headphones so that they could converse. A seasoned traveler in the chopper, Buffy had already fastened hers around her head.

"Hello, Buff," he said into his mouthpiece as soon as Diana had her earphones in place.

"Hi yourself, captain. I was wondering when you were going to notice I was alive."

He grinned. "Sorry... your friend distracted me."

"That's obvious." Buffy's voice crackled over the wire. "I say more power to both of you, provided you can concentrate sufficiently to keep this contraption in the air!"

"I'll do my damnedest."

Glancing at Rafe, Diana could see he hadn't really expected Buffy to disapprove of them. Clearly, though, he'd wanted her blessing as Diana's oldest friend. He'd like the whole world to know and be pleased that we're lovers, she thought. So would I—if it weren't for the terrible problems we'd have to face.

It took them about twenty minutes to cross the hundred and fifty miles or so of arid Indian land that stretched between Tuba City and the remote area north of the Utah line where the screening would take place.

Rafe brought the chopper down near a well, a cluster of dusty trees and an adobe building that marked a small trading post. One look at the stony dirt track that led up to it and she knew why they'd come by air.

"This is it," he said, taking the earphones off and turning to her. "Magic Butte. I thought you'd want to know. Some of your relatives may attend the clinic today."

An odd thrill came over her at the thought. Swiftly, she glanced behind her to see if Buffy had overheard. But the rotor blades were still turning slowly, and Buffy had her back to them as she unloaded their supplies.

"I guess you haven't told her about being related to these people," Rafe said.

"Actually I mentioned it just this morning. I really haven't had much time to explain."

"Does that mean you believe me now?"

Picking up her physician's bag and lab coat, Diana shrugged her shoulders. "I *want* to believe you, if that's any comfort," she said. "But my father denies it. And I haven't enough evidence to decide one way or the other yet. Maybe I'll just know the truth when I see these cousins of mine...if they decide to come today."

They set up the clinic in a storeroom at the trading post that had been partially emptied for the purpose. A table and some folding chairs had been put out for them and there was a small bathroom. Several family groups—mostly mothers or grandmothers and small children—had arrived early to wait for them. Little by little, more people drifted in. They soon found themselves with their hands full, just as they had the week before at the Tuba City hospital.

Each dark-eyed, straight-haired child who stripped to the waist to be examined and have a T.B. scratch test done on his or her arm made Diana wonder afresh if here was a small kinsman, descended like her from Annie Little Joe. But she was concentrating on her work and couldn't give it much thought.

Then Rafe, who'd been helping the makeshift clinic's visitors to fill out forms, came over to speak quietly to her. "They're here," he said, nodding at the door where a stolid, graying woman in her mid-forties had just entered with two youngsters. One of them was a girl in her early teens, pretty and shy. The other, a boy of about ten who had a black eye, appeared to be recovering from a fistfight.

"The woman is named Mary Flatbow," he told her. "She's the children's grandmother and Josh's second cousin. The children—Johnny and Daisy—are from her daughter Rozanne's first marriage."

If Mary Flatbow was Josh's second cousin, she would be one quarter white. Diana looked at them silently for a moment, trying to see something of Josh in them, or herself. She was sorry to admit that to her they looked like any other Indians.

"Please introduce them to me when their turn comes," she asked, searching awkwardly for the correct protocol.

He raised one level brow. "As your cousins?"

"You might as well."

Several families were ahead of the Flatbows and it was nearly a quarter of an hour before the Indian woman and her grandchildren reached the head of the line.

Informally Rafe made the introductions. Mary Flatbow acknowledged them, giving Diana a swift, black-eyed glance and then casting down her eyes, as if she'd always known of the connection but didn't want to admit her curiosity.

Like her, Daisy continued to stare at the floor. Johnny, brown and compact, quite a handsome child really, stared Diana impassively in the face.

"I'm glad to meet you," she replied forthrightly, taking the grandmother's rough brown hand. "What happened to your grandson? It looks like he's been in quite a fight."

"He got hurt." Still Mary wouldn't meet her eyes. Apparently the terse admission exhausted the store of information she was willing to impart.

Passing Daisy along to Buffy for the T.B. test, Diana asked the boy to take off his shirt. Frowningly she examined the boy's bare torso, which was covered with welts and bruises. With delicate, knowledgeable fingers, she probed for broken bones and sighed with relief when there weren't any. Still, it was obvious he'd suffered a severe beating and recently, too.

"How did this happen?" she asked again, getting out her first-aid kit. "These aren't the kinds of injuries you get at school or play."

Predictably, Johnny didn't answer her either. And Mary Flatbow stubbornly refused to speak. Diana was about to demand that Rafe question her in the Navaho language when Daisy blurted, "Jim did it."

"Who's Jim?" Diana asked.

Her spurt of courage waning, Daisy hung her head.

After much prodding, Mary turned to Rafe and spoke a few sentences in her native tongue.

"She says Jim Fox, the boy's stepfather, beats him regularly, that he's knocked him unconscious several times," Rafe related. "He's trouble...known for getting in fights both here and in every town for miles around. The mother is pregnant right now and afraid of him. I don't think he wants another male, particularly some other man's son, in the household."

"But that's terrible!" Diana was visibly shocked. "The boy could be killed. Why hasn't someone gone to the police or the district attorney? There's a law against beating children!"

At the other end of the long table, Buffy paused to stare at them. Johnny regarded Diana stoically. He was well able to understand their rapid exchange in English, she was certain. He looked at her as if convinced there was nothing she could or would do about the situation.

Rafe laid one hand lightly yet restrainingly on Diana's shoulder. "I'll explain it in a minute, when you're finished with Johnny," he said.

Still furious about the welts that marked the boy's slight brown frame, she reddened, embarrassed to be caught talking about him in his presence. "All right," she conceded, remembering what Buffy had told her about the dignity of these people. "Thanks . . . for reminding me to shut my mouth."

When finally she'd finished with the iodine bottle and bandages and Johnny was reporting to Buffy for the skin prick, Rafe drew her aside.

"First of all," he explained, "tribal justice rules here on the reservation. Its seat is at Window Rock, many miles distant. As you can see, the Flatbows live in a remote isolated area. Roads are poor at best, and—when it rains or snows—nonexistent. The stepfather's beat-up truck is the only vehicle in the family."

"Well . . . couldn't someone else have stepped in then? A relative or a neighbor?"

"You don't understand. Since Navaho society is matriarchal, tradition holds that Mary's male relatives must keep James Fox in line. Unfortunately, there aren't any men left among her close kin . . . except for your father."

Breathing fire, Diana didn't stop to consider the consequences. "Fine," she snapped, her concern for

Johnny pushing her across the threshold of belief in Rafe's contention that she had Indian blood. "If my father won't shoulder his responsibility to these people, then I will. I'm taking Johnny home with me until I get this situation straightened out to my satisfaction."

She was a physician, after all—one who'd been taught in medical school that the patient's welfare came first and that she was the arbiter of what that meant.

"Sweetheart—" Rafe shook his head "—you can't just walk away with him."

"Then explain what I want to his grandmother. If this is a matriarchal culture, she has the authority to let him go. And if she loves him or cares in the slightest about his safety, that's just what she'll do."

Rafe seemed astonished and a little bemused at the depth of her determination. But she could tell that though he clearly felt the idea was an impractical one, he admired her for proposing it.

"Now that I know about this, I can go to Window Rock on Johnny's behalf myself," he suggested. "That is, if I can convince Mary or her daughter to swear out a complaint."

Diana glanced at the square, uncommunicative Mary. "You can tell that's not likely," she surmised. "Anyway...in the meantime, Johnny could be killed." Each time she mentioned the boy's name, she could feel him watching her with those shiny, opaque eyes. "Talk to Mary about this in her own language," she urged. "You can make her understand."

Her dark-haired lover considered. "I can try," he said at last. "She might let him go for a brief visit if I say it's to meet your father."

If his remark was intended to bring her back to reality, it had the desired effect. But her personal inclination and her training to help and protect others, particularly a child, were too strong for her to back off for personal considerations.

"You're right—my father will raise holy hell," she admitted. "But I'm not going to let someone kill that boy."

Rafe sighed. "All right, Diana. If you feel so strongly, I'll do my best. But you'd better be prepared to bring Johnny to me...and maybe come to stay yourself...if things don't work out quite the way you've planned."

Somehow, perhaps through the very considerable force of his personality, he managed to convince Mary Flatbow to let her grandson come for a three-day visit with his blond doctor cousin. She caught a brief glimpse of astonishment in Johnny's eyes before he shuttered all emotion. But he didn't argue. His grandmother's word, she guessed, was law to him.

Mary wasn't so cooperative when Diana, sensing that the boy's grandmother was ill, offered to give her a checkup as well. "Not sick," said the Indian woman, her words belying her unhealthy color and the dark circles Diana had noted beneath her eyes.

Johnny couldn't hide his thrilled fascination with the helicopter or keep from craning his neck as they soared away from Magic Butte late that afternoon. He seemed much less taken with the idea of getting into Diana's Wagoneer at the Tuba City airport, particularly since that meant he would be separated from Rafe.

Yet he entered the vehicle obediently enough.

"I'll pick up some clothes for him in town," Diana told Rafe as they said goodbye at the edge of the landing strip.

"You plan on keeping him more than three days, don't you?"

She nodded. "I know the district attorney, or at least Josh does. But he's a hard man to reach and I'd rather not go through Del unless I must. It'll take some time, also, to get a social worker to investigate the case. But as far as I'm concerned, Johnny doesn't go back to Magic Butte until James Fox is in custody."

There was a small silence. "What's this going to mean for us, Diana?" her black-eyed man questioned. "When are we going to have some time alone?"

She shook her head. "I don't know," she admitted. "I won't be able to leave Johnny by himself out at the ranch for the first few days."

The Indian boy watched them from the Wagoneer as they came together in a fierce embrace, and then let each other go.

On the way back to the Double Bar B, he sat in stony silence. Diana, consumed with her own worries and aching at even a temporary denial of Rafe's company didn't coax him to break it.

Finally, as they turned off the interstate and headed down the dust-clouded private road that wound back onto the Bailey property, he spoke. "Is Rafe . . . your man?" he asked in a small voice from the opposite side of the leather bench seat.

"Yes, he is." She threw him a swift glance.

"And are you really my cousin?"

The relative truth or falsehood of the conflicting stories she'd heard didn't seem to matter now. "Yes,

Johnny,'' she replied without hesitation. "That's why I won't let anything like this happen to you again."

As they parked out by the corral, she thought it best to warn Johnny his Uncle Josh had been ill and sometimes behaved irrationally. "You may not be able to spend much time with him until he's feeling better," she said. "There'll be plenty for you to do. I'll ask our ranch hand, Billy, to find you a horse to ride."

At her mention of a horse, she was rewarded with the hesitant glimmer of a smile. She took the precaution of bringing Johnny in through the kitchen, and leaving him with Mrs. Purdy, who quickly provided cookies, milk and a grandmotherly presence.

Predictably, Josh was furious when she confronted him in his study and explained the situation. "I won't have a Navaho brat about the place!" he roared, so angrily Diana feared she would have to give him a tranquilizer to avert another stroke.

"He'll only be here a short time for his own protection until I can get a social worker lined up to investigate the case," she insisted, hoping her calm behavior would have a soothing effect. "I know you won't admit to it, but there's some question he might be a relative of ours. Even if he's not I couldn't just leave him to his fate."

Josh swore but didn't really answer her. He probably understood that the alternative was for her to take Johnny elsewhere and remain absent herself.

"You don't have to see him if you don't want to," she added. "Mrs. Purdy and Billy can look after him."

To make sure things went smoothly Diana stayed close to the ranch for several days, mollifying her father with extra attention and watching Johnny follow ranch hand Billy Shaw about as he gentled a foal. She was out riding with the boy on Thursday afternoon when Rafe finally called. Mrs. Purdy gave her the message as they came in. Sending Johnny into the den to watch television, a luxury to which he'd rapidly adapted, she slipped away to the privacy of her room.

Rafe hadn't left his name, just a number. As she dialed it, she realized he'd remained anonymous for her sake though it must have gone against his pride.

Not surprisingly, he asked how things were going. Then he insisted, "I want to see you, just to hold you in my arms. You've made it awfully hard for me, darling, to do without you."

It went without saying that she felt the same. Unfortunately, Friday was the start of the Labor Day weekend and the day of the dress rehearsal for Buffy's Saturday wedding. A party had been scheduled afterward at the Fairfield Country Club. As maid of honor, Diana naturally was obliged to attend both events.

"We probably won't be able to get together until Sunday at the earliest," she said regretfully, going on to explain.

"You could always bring a guest tomorrow night," he suggested in his offhand way.

Clearly it was a request for her to go public with their relationship. "I'm not sure I should," she answered. "My father..."

"He'll have to accept the fact of our relationship sooner or later. I know what I said that day out at the creek. But I don't plan to go on making love to you like a thief in the night."

The brief flash of pride and temper only made her want him more.

"Of course, you should take whatever safeguards you feel are necessary for your father's health," he added. "But you can't let his illness rule you. You're a doctor. You know he could live with this condition for years."

Rafe was right, of course. She realized suddenly that she was afraid—not just for her father's sake, but for her own. It didn't bother her that taking Rafe to the rehearsal and the party afterward would probably shock her friends; yet she knew it was another step toward losing the only parent she'd ever really known.

Rafe was asking her to step off the rim of a canyon and believe that he could catch her. There was only one argument on his side, but it was a powerful one, her strong love for him. "All right," she said, taking that step into thin air. "I'll have to talk to him first. Can you pick me up at the house on Mount Pleasant Road about four o'clock?"

The line was silent for a moment. "And after the party?" Rafe asked.

Any hesitation she still had dissolved at the need in his voice. "You can take me to a place where the rest of the world can't reach us," she suggested, "and make wildly sustained love to me."

Josh was livid when she explained that Rafe would be her escort for the evening. "I thought I'd tell you myself before one of your sources got to you with the news," she said.

He choked. "My daughter and a half-breed! I absolutely forbid..."

Calmly she took his blood pressure. "You don't have that right. Please keep your voice down. I don't want Johnny to hear."

He grunted. "The boy's back outside with Billy, helping break in that damn foal."

To her surprise, Josh's tone had softened when he spoke about Johnny. As if he'd noted it too, he immediately made up for the lapse with a string of expletives aimed at Rafe. With difficulty, Diana refrained from defending the man she loved and thus making her father even angrier.

"Rafe and I are friends," she said in her best this-subject-is-closed voice. "I plan to see him while I'm here."

It wasn't a totally honest ploy, because her plans to remain in Flagstaff had stretched to the indefinite. But perhaps because she seemed to hint that nothing permanent could come of the relationship, Josh calmed down more quickly than she'd had any right to hope. His opinion hadn't changed one iota, though, she guessed. There was no way to tell—without asking—whether the dislike of Indians he harbored stemmed from his wife's betrayal.

Rafe called for her in a dark suit, white shirt and burgundy tie that set off his dramatic good looks. "You look beautiful, darling," he said, his dark eyes raking over her emerald-green silk dress and coming to rest on the curve of bosom revealed by its deeply cut neckline. "That outfit does what I'd like to do... follow the curves of your body."

"It's silk," Diana said. "Go ahead and touch it. I wore it especially for you."

For several moments she didn't think they'd get out of the Queen Anne foyer at all—except to climb the stairs to her bed. "Let's go," he told her, catching his breath. "I took you at your word and planned something very special for us tonight."

On the way to Nativity Church Diana racked her brain, trying to guess what he had in mind. When they parked the car near the church door, though, she couldn't help but shift her attention to the way her friends would react. She could picture the stir their arrival was going to cause—the stares, the quickly spreading tide of whispers.

She wasn't much mistaken. Introductions were politely acknowledged, but only just, by people she'd known for years. Obviously aware of what was going on but appearing faintly amused by it, Rafe took a seat by himself in the back pew as the rehearsal began. A bit less self-contained about it than he, Diana was feeling very annoyed on his behalf as she stepped into line beside Del, Rob's best man.

During the minutes since their arrival, her former date's initial shock had given way to outrage, jealousy and despairing looks.

"I can't believe this is what you want, Diana," he told her in a low and furious tone. "But at least I can see now why you haven't had time for me."

There didn't seem to be any answer she could give without antagonizing him further. She could feel Rafe's eyes on her and did her best to feign nonchalance. Just the same, the attitude of her old friends and acquaintances had given her pause. If this were our wedding and our rehearsal, would any of these people attend? she wondered. Would we be better advised to drive over to Williams or Prescott and have some justice of the peace marry us?

At the club, Diana wanted to pull Rafe aside into the cozy bar with its tub chairs, soft lights and intimate dance floor. She barely suppressed the urge as they walked on past it, hand in hand through the dining area, to the Fairfield Room with its cold, formal blue-and-gray striped satin chairs, pianist playing cocktail music and crowd of people she knew.

It could be worse, she thought, looking at the red, flat mesa beyond the golf greens, with the foothills of the San Francisco peaks in the distance. At least there's a view, even if we can't ignore everyone and look only at it.

With effort, she put on her most sociable face and linked her arm through that of the man she loved. "C'mon, darling," she said, loudly enough to be overheard. "Let's get a drink. There are some other people I want you to meet."

He knew most of them, though in a different context, of course. Now that the initial shock had worn off, the majority were behaving like the gracious, well-brought-up adults she'd thought them to be. They could find nothing to quarrel with in Rafe's behavior. Polite and urbane, he was hardly the dusty, uneducated sheepherder the more prejudiced among them might have expected. Only Del, keeping the room between them, continued to glower at the two of them.

Ultimately, she wasn't too surprised when several of the women unbent enough to flirt with her escort. He's the best-looking man here, she thought, with far and away the most sex appeal. They're probably wondering what it's like to sleep with him.

Buffy and Rob arrived late—so obviously happy that it made tears well in Diana's eyes. Her friend's hair was mussed and Rob's eyes were glinting with pleasure. Probably they'd been making out in the parking lot, she thought. This evening's hassle had been worth it, just to share this moment in my best friend's life.

Buffy's eyes lit when she saw Diana on Rafe's arm. Quickly she drew them to the forefront of the party— obviously pleased that Diana had seen fit to go public with the romance.

Later, there were pictures taken. Diana and Del had to pose together with the wedding party in front of the windows. Hugging Buffy when they were finished, Diana initiated a rapid, whispered exchange. A moment later she went to Rafe and laced her hand through his. "I asked Buff if it would be all right for us to leave now," she whispered.

"And?" he asked, his dark eyes full of promise.

"I won't repeat her answer word for word. But it translated to yes."

They pulled away from the club in his pickup truck, their arms about each other. The awkwardness with her friends forgotten, Diana was thinking only of the night ahead and where he would take her.

"I hope you brought your outdoor things," he said with a little growl, caressing her through the thin silk of her gown. "Much as I like that dress, it won't do for what I have in mind tonight."

Eight

Luckily, she'd tucked jeans, a Western shirt and a jacket into her overnight bag. "I don't suppose you'd want to tell me what that is," she murmured, nestling against his shoulder.

Rafe slipped his hand into her neckline. "Not yet," he replied, taking his eyes off the road momentarily to brush her temple with a kiss. Beneath her emerald silk bodice, his strong, lean fingers were lightly exploring one breast, caressing its tight, aroused bud.

Half reeling at his touch and the delicious, erotic scent of him, she could feel the hard muscles of his chest and shoulders through the dark, expensively tailored suit jacket. "Can you know what it does when you put your hands on me that way?" she whispered.

"I know what it makes me feel." He paused. "Do you realize, *querida*, we've been lacking each other a lifetime? And that since we finally made love, it's been less than a week? Each day that passed, I was aching to hold you."

It took them only a short time via the interstate and Route 89A to reach his ranch. Shutting off the ignition, Rafe put both arms around her. Covering her mouth with his, he gave her such a rapacious and deeply loving kiss that she wanted to cry.

"Here...in the truck?" she managed, not quite trusting her emotions.

He grinned. "No, but we'll have to try that sometime. Remember? You wanted a place where the rest of the world couldn't reach us. Let's go in and change. If we don't hurry, we'll lose the sunset."

They entered his bedroom through the sliding glass door as she had a week earlier. Again she thought how well this private retreat fitted him as a person, with its beautiful rugs hanging from the walls like works of art, the huge fieldstone hearth and his archaeologist's collection of Indian pottery and artifacts displayed on a lighted wall.

It felt a little funny, putting her overnight bag down beside his bed and standing there facing him, matter-of-factly unbuttoning her dress. How will we be able to stop ourselves from making love right here? she wondered, laying the dress out carefully on the sheepskin coverlet and taking off her stockings. Because I know that's what my body is yearning for.

Standing there barefoot in her beige charmeuse teddy, she watched with softly parted lips as Rafe took off his suit and shirt. The way his muscles moved under their smooth, warm covering of bronze-colored skin made her want to kiss and touch him everywhere.

His eyes were devouring her too. Zipping up his jeans, he stepped closer to fondle her through the satiny texture of her undergarment.

"Not here," he told her after a moment, "even though neither of us might want to wait. I really do have a special place in mind."

Quickly donning her jeans and shirt, she slipped her feet into worn, comfortable loafers. "Ready," she announced, grabbing up her jacket.

"I have everything else we'll need in the chopper," he said. "Let's go."

There was a cooler in the helicopter's back seat, along with a down-filled sleeping bag, a bundle of split oak and some other camping supplies. Already, behind the darkened spires of the pointed pines, the sun had suffused the sky with rose, magenta and the tenderest shade of gold.

Diana took her place beside Rafe, and like a veteran flier, now quickly fastened on her headphones. They rose above the ranch into the sky's symphony of colors, its panorama of glowing clouds. Rafe took her hand and laid it on his knee as they tilted away toward the south and the sheer drop of the Oak Creek switchbacks. It wasn't a moment for conversation, but their shared pleasure in the rapidly deepening hues that surrounded them was easily communicated in the language of touch.

If she'd thought the head of the canyon was beautiful on horseback, this time she was overwhelmed. From their vantage point the dying sun's pyrotechnics echoed from one sheer, pine-clad cliff to the other with all the splendid harmony of musical counterpoint. It was only a matter of minutes before the canyon widened below them, emptying the dark line of syca-

mores that marked the creek into Sedona's stunning
high-desert valley of red rock cliffs and monuments.

A deep, velvety purple was swallowing up the most
incendiary color as they swung off sharply to the left
toward a mass of red sandstone that guarded the rim
of the canyon but stood apart.

"I doubt if anyone will disturb us here," Rafe said
casually, setting the chopper down. "They'd need
rappeling gear and one hell of a lot of determination."

Awed by the place he had chosen, Diana stepped out
onto the stony ground. Gradually the chopper blades
slowed and then hung motionless, granting them the
soft evening sounds that were their own special kind
of silence. As they stood facing west, the sun's last rays
glowed at the edge of rock towers and formations that
were similar to theirs. A great horned owl gave its dis-
tinctive call, the sound echoing and reechoing. Below
them, the lights of Sedona twinkled on, one by one, as
if someone had carelessly flung down a handful of
diamonds.

"Will it do, Cornsilk Woman?" Rafe asked, coming up to put his arms around her from behind.

"Perfectly," she said. To her, their landing place
was a breathtaking aerie, a trysting place for the gods.
My life has opened out like this canyon since he found
me again, she thought. I've never seen vistas like these
before, or felt myself to be such a part of the uni-
verse. Yet, in a sense my world has narrowed too;
everything in it, now, focuses on him.

Turning, she slipped her arms about Rafe's neck.
Her fingers were buried in his thick, dark hair. "It's
time I let you know the truth about something," she
said. "I love you very much."

"Ah, Diana..."

When his tongue invaded her moist depths, she let herself sway a little, knowing he wouldn't let her fall. Each time they touched, it seemed, they moved closer and closer together, until they must become one person; their separate halves blended so completely they could never draw apart.

Yet, with all her being she desired an even closer union. She wanted the ecstasy of having him inside her. "Let's get out the sleeping bag," she urged, unbuttoning his shirt.

"The temperature's already dropping," he told her. "We'll have to build a fire."

Knowing him as she did now, she realized he also wanted to prolong the anticipation. "I'll help," she offered, turning toward the chopper to get out supplies.

He'd been right, earlier, when he'd said a week wasn't long compared with the years they'd spent apart. Yet just to brush against him now as they unloaded their gear was sweet torture. She was tingling with anticipation to the soles of her feet as she zipped the two halves of his double sleeping bag together and they took turns blowing up the heavy army-surplus air mattress that would cushion them from the ground.

Light and shadow played on Rafe's aquiline features and partially bared chest as the bonfire blazed up in the deepening shadows. In that setting, he looked almost totally Indian.

A chill passed over his skin when she put her hand inside the opened front of his shirt. "You're still wearing your jacket, sweetheart," he noted, his voice both abrasive and tender. "If you're going to undress me, you'll have to keep me warm."

The idea of stripping him down to his smooth, coppery skin there in the carmine glow of the firelight was an aphrodisiac to her senses. "Don't doubt that I'll do it, Coyote Man," she said, running her palms over the beautifully formed muscles of his shoulders and upper arms as she removed the shirt altogether.

Working her way down his splendid torso with little kisses, she took off his belt. Then came the snap on his waistband and the rasp of his zipper as she parted it and caressed his lower abdomen, her fingers brushing against his crisp body hair.

Rafe's hips were arrow straight and she slid his jeans easily to the ground. With a little exclamation of pleasure, she covered his hard desire with her hand. If the women at the club could see him now, she thought—or even imagine what it's like to welcome the fire of his touch. How they'd envy me, and lust after my dark-haired savage, my handsome, well-educated man.

High overhead, several planes winked red against the darkness. Doubtless they were part of a fighter wing on training orders from the base in Phoenix, racing for home. The fire they'd built atop the sheer precipice would definitely attract attention from the air. Could the unseen pilots pick them out, standing there beside Rafe's chopper, a woman in jeans and shirt and jacket, caressing her naked lover?

"Now you, Diana," Rafe said, the corners of his mouth turning down a little as if he could read her thoughts.

"Yes," she murmured. "Yes."

Yet for a moment she wouldn't relinquish him as her free hand smoothed the hard planes of his back to capture his narrow, bunching buttocks, the faintly hairy curve of his upper thighs.

Then their fingers were meeting at her buttons and zipper placket and she was kicking her jeans aside, slithering the fragile silk teddy from her body. Though they stood near the fire, the cold night air hit her in a rush. She noticed it only absently, burning as she was for his love.

"Let me take you, beloved," he urged, grasping her gently by the nipples and pulling her back into his embrace. His tender grip as he claimed her delicate peaks left her defenseless. "Oh, yes, Rafael," she whispered. "I want you so."

Standing there with him on that height, wrapped in the darkened cloak of sky with its embroidery of stars, was like being poised at the very brink of creation. The feeling went far beyond the physical dimension. What we have at this moment is more than most people share in a lifetime, she thought—something so precious that, if anything should happen to separate us, it would leave a wound as wide as this canyon in my heart.

"I was wrong," he said, shaking his head as he looked down at her with love. "You're not some lesser spirit, but Changing Woman herself..."

"Who is Changing Woman?" The words came out of her like a breath.

"The female spirit of creation." His voice almost reverent, he began to speak in what she guessed were the rhythms of an ancient chant.

"Now at the summit of Gobernador Knob he found her, Talking God found her, ni yo 'o. Dark cloud, white water and rainbow were there. The corn beetle

called out with its pretty voice. Before her it was blessed, behind her it was blessed..."

His hands moved down her torso, skimming her pelvic bones.

"*... when he found her, when he found her,* ni yo 'o.*"

He added three more words in the Navaho tongue that sounded like *sahanaray bekay hozhon.* "That means something like 'ultimate beauty and peace,'" he translated, "the feeling a man and a woman have when they're resting from their love."

Bending down, he unzipped one corner of the quilted bag and folded it back so that they could climb inside. Wrapped in its light, cuddly warmth, their bodies converged with a sweetness that was part relief and part mounting passion. Lying atop her, Rafe left their shoulders temporarily exposed to the night air so that he could lower his head to her breast.

They wouldn't be able to draw the preliminaries out for long, she knew, exquisite sensations knifing through her as he pushed up her ivory swell, the better to suckle its responsive bud. He'd found their time apart as difficult as she, that was certain, especially the moment when they'd had to let go of each other at the Tuba City airport so she could take Johnny home. Just the beloved weight of his body now, pressing on hers after that hiatus, was enough to make her wild.

It really *is* like that day at the creek, she decided, the little sounds made by his mouth fueling her longing. Except that now we're naked together. I should have known that if he ever touched me, I'd always be his.

His mouth warm and tender, Rafe trailed his kisses from one breast to the other, rubbing the hard, wet nipple he'd abandoned between forefinger and thumb.

Instinctively her most feminine places throbbed to receive him.

"I can't wait for you much longer," he admitted, moving up so that his breath feathered against her mouth.

"You don't have to."

In response, he parted her legs with one hard knee and laced his fingers through hers. A moment later he lay between her thighs and she could feel his seeking. Unable to guide him with her hands, she tilted forward to position her soft privacy for his entry, offering everything she had and everything she was.

His first deep thrust nearly set her off in a shower of sparks. For a moment, he remained very still, as if he'd almost lost control himself, the fullness of him seeming to pervade her soul. Once again she was part of him, part of her lost self, so enmeshed in his being that she could almost think his thoughts.

"I have all of you, Diana," he whispered, his voice almost unrecognizable with emotion.

"As I want you to."

Beginning slowly, their movement seemed orchestrated by the gods—driven, surely, by a force too powerful and elemental to stem from mortal passion. From the depths of her nature, Diana gave to him and gave. Caught up in the legend he'd recited, she raged to be his Changing Woman, the dimly understood combination of earth mother and Navaho goddess who served willingly as the altar of his need.

Inevitably the pleasure was too sharp, too pervasive to last. She was the first to rocket free from all restraint, her knees open wide and her feet clinging to the ground for purchase as she met the full force of their consummation. Shivers broke over her like waves, even as a warm deluge of satisfaction claimed her. He followed almost instantly, crying out against the softness of her shoulder.

Drifting down like a falling spark, Diana felt carried out of herself and somehow changed. Already there's more love between us than I dreamed could exist in the world, she thought. I won't be able to do without him again.

Above them, the bright desert moon had made its appearance, flooding the canyon's rock pinnacles and fortresses with milky light. Rolling off her, Rafe drew her back into the circle of his arm.

"You mean everything to me," he said simply, kissing her damp brow as if to seal what they had shared.

"My sweet Rafael... I love you so much."

They were silent a moment, just holding each other. "It's so close to heaven on this rock," Diana added, gazing up at the sky.

His little grumble of assent was close beside her ear. "Here and everywhere," he told her, "that you let me love you to sleep."

They awoke to sunshine and the distant sounds of Labor Day weekend traffic winding between Flagstaff and Sedona, flowing on toward Camp Verde or Jerome. The intrusions of the real world surrounded them—still at bay, perhaps, but definitely a factor again.

"I don't want to leave you," Diana complained, stretching the kinks out of her neck and shoulders and curling back into his arms.

The little line beside his mouth deepened. "Isn't Buffy getting married today?"

"As a matter of fact, she is."

"I seem to remember that you're the maid of honor, *querida*. You have to go."

"Then come with me." Lovingly she nibbled at his ear.

To her surprise, Rafe refused to comply with her wishes. "I can't help but think that, yesterday, I was testing you," he admitted. "It's my damn pride. I love you, Diana, but I want more from you than your stolen moments. I want to be someone you introduce to your friends as the man with whom you plan to spend a lifetime."

"Oh, Rafe..." Her hands framing the hard line of his jaw, she tried to cover his mouth with hers.

"No...let me finish," he interposed. "It would be too easy to use lovemaking as an argument, let it persuade you to do something you'd regret. Go to the wedding, darling, and think about what Buffy and Rob are promising each other. Come back to me later if that's what you want for us."

Diana was pierced to the heart with a mixture of joy and trepidation. He was asking for everything—the sacrifice of her fellowship and the promise of a life together.

If that were all, it would be easy, she thought. Josh is unreasonable to hate every Indian who walks the face of this earth even if Max's story is true. And it's probably his overly concerned daughter, not the sensible Dr. Diana Bailey, who's worried about causing another cerebrovascular accident if she goes against his wishes.

What was reasonable and what actually *was*, unfortunately, were two different things. She might very well end up losing her father forever and breaking his heart if she insisted on keeping the man she loved.

Rafe's right about one thing, she thought; it wouldn't be fair, either to him or to Josh, if I tried to make a hasty choice. At that moment, she was half on the verge of telling him Max's story as they lay there in each other's arms. He would have to hear it eventually if they were to fight Josh's prejudice together. Still, she decided against it for the moment, unwilling that he should take responsibility for a problem that was rightly hers.

"If I'm going to the wedding, I have to get up and dress," she reminded him, striving for a light tone. "But it's broad daylight. Someone is sure to see us."

"Then we'll have to put our things on some-how...inside the bag." All seriousness departing his dark eyes as if it had never been, he reached for their clothing. "I'm afraid the process may be awkward...and more than a little intimate, Diana. They may have to hold up the ceremony for you after all."

She was on time for Buffy's wedding, but only just. The ceremony was traditional and beautiful, with all the lace and candlelight and misty-eyed friends they had imagined as girls together. Wildly in love herself and caught up in the sentiment of the occasion, Diana stood by while her oldest chum softly made her vows. All the commitment Rafe had been talking about was clearly there as Buffy looked up at Rob with shining eyes, all the certainty that this man's love was what she wanted above all else in the world.

It's easy for her, Diana thought, envying her friend. Max approves of Rob, and he welcomed him into the family. Josh would never accept Rafe that way. He'd cut himself off from me—even though, when I was growing up, each of us was the only family that the other had.

I still have that significance for Josh, she realized. Meanwhile, her love for Rafe had grown stronger until it filled her whole being, threatening to relegate family loyalties to second place.

As the priest pronounced Buffy and Rob man and wife, a phrase Diana remembered from Sunday-school lessons ran through her mind. *Whither thou goest, I will go,* a woman named Ruth had said. *Thy people shall be my people...*

She laid the choice Rafe had posed her aside in her heart as the ceremony ended. Let the decision make itself, she thought as Rob and Buffy kissed. Moments later, she and Del preceded the newly married couple out into the sunlight. Brimming with emotion, she helped pelt the happy pair with rice and tried to ignore the awkwardness that had sprung up between herself and her former beau.

But she couldn't ignore him at the reception in the parish hall, though she didn't dance with him. Just after an exuberant Buffy tossed her bouquet of white roses and baby's breath directly into Diana's hands, Del stepped close to whisper in her ear.

"I notice you didn't bring your squaw man today," he said. "Does that mean last night was just a gesture of rebellion against your father?"

For Diana, his remark was the catalyst she'd been seeking. Not even angry she turned to Del, knowing suddenly what she wanted to do.

"Rafe Marquez means everything to me," she said, her gray eyes meeting his so straightforwardly that he couldn't mistake her meaning. "I'd appreciate it if you'd speak of him with more respect."

Del's face crumpled. Not waiting for an answer, she put several paces between them and turned to watch Buffy and Rob ride away together in Rob's new imported car. My blessings on both of you, she told them silently, her hopes and wishes winging after them. Thanks to your example, I'm going to step off into an even bigger chasm this afternoon, with only my love to guide me.

Rafe was smoking by the corral when she turned in at his gate, the bouquet of white roses and baby's breath beside her on the seat. He threw away his cigarette and stood there watching her as she parked the car and came toward him across the stable yard.

How beautiful he is, she thought, running her eyes over his straight black hair, admiring the way his broad shoulders filled out his old plaid shirt and his slim muscular legs were outlined by his worn and faded jeans. And how lucky I am to have him. I love him down to the soles of his dusty boots.

"Rafe," she whispered, halting before him almost as a suppliant.

He didn't take hold of her hands. "I wasn't sure you'd come," he answered slowly. "After what I said this morning..."

"You really thought I could stay away?"

He gave a little shrug. A question shone forth in his dark eyes though he didn't let himself ask it.

"I love you," Diana reminded him, letting go of her last firm foothold. "You haven't exactly asked me yet, but I want to marry you and have your children. We'll have to face more problems than you even realize. I'm going to need time..."

Joy leaped in his beautiful eyes, but he didn't put his emotions into the fragile substance of words. Instead, Rafe Marquez—friend, lover and guide figure of her past—simply enfolded her in his arms.

Nine

Diana wasn't sure how long they stood, holding fast to each other in the bright afternoon. She could almost feel the earth turning through the soles of her feet as she pressed herself against the man she'd just promised to love for a lifetime, a man who was as essential to her now as sunlight and breath.

Then Rafe's favorite saddle horse, Yebetchai, nickered softly and thrust his velvet nose over the corral fence. Digging into his pocket, Rafe handed over the desired lump of sugar. Giving the stallion's nose a pat, he turned to look deep into Diana's eyes.

"I have a load of fresh hay in the shed," he suggested, love and lust warring beneath the dark fringe of his lashes. "If it would please you, I could make a sweet-smelling place for us to lie down together."

Longing shot through her at the image he evoked.
"You know how much that would please me, Rafael," she whispered.

Their arms twined about each other, they walked
into the tack and hay barn together. Except for a few
slanting rays of light it was quite dim inside its corrugated tin and frame walls. The combined scents of
saddle leather and fresh hay pleasantly assailed
Diana's nostrils. She noted a pile of rough saddle
blankets and various types of harness. Sacks of feed,
probably oats, were piled in a corner.

Rearranging several bales and breaking one open to
spread it about, Rafe smoothed one of the blankets in
place. "I can't believe you're really mine," he told her,
shaking his head. "Or that we'll have children together. They'll be brown as nuts, darling, with my
black hair."

"I'll love them all the more for that," she said.

Suddenly it seemed the height of incongruity that
she was standing in that rustic shelter in her formal
gown, or that she was even wearing anything at all.
While he watched with slightly parted lips, she
stripped off the dressmaker's pale-green creation and
her lacy underthings and stood facing him with his
silver coyote ring on its chain her only ornament.

He didn't ask her to take it off and slip it onto her
finger as she knew he'd like to do. She'd requested
time to settle things with her father and he character-
istically respected her wishes.

But there was nothing restrained or hesitant about
the way he took her that afternoon. He pulled her
down atop him on the hay-cushioned blanket without
even taking off his own clothing. Her hair fanning out
about her face and her breasts compressed against

him, she leaned down to kiss his mouth. Little brush-fires ignited in her blood as he ran his hands over her body.

Each time they'd made love before, he'd tried to wait, drawing out the sweet suspense of it until they both reached the breaking point. Now she knew without being told that he was following his Indian grandfather's dictum, and setting an immediate seal on their bargain.

Letting go of her momentarily, he unzipped his jeans and pulled them down just far enough to free his desire. Able to grasp him this time, she fitted him inside her, exclaiming as she did so at the depth to which he filled her emptiness.

When it exploded this time, their release was so profound that it seemed to shake the earth. "Mine," Diana gasped, collapsing against him as the heat spread through her body. "You're mine, Rafael Marquez...mine to keep."

Though it was nearly supper time, it was still relatively warm in the shed as they quieted. Rolling onto her back, Diana curled into the protective hollow of his shoulder. For a little while they just lay there, spent and drowsy.

When at last the cooler air of dusk prompted them to get up, he redressed her lovingly. "Come into the house, and I'll make you a fire," he promised. "I have some juniper wood that will burn for us all night long."

Rafe was surprised when, later that week, Diana told him her father had accepted her postponement of the fellowship readily enough.

"I can't leave you just now, Dad," she'd told Josh as they sat together on the patio, gazing off toward the peaks where a distant thunderstorm was disgorging feathery torrents of gray.

"Hell, you're hardly ever home, girl," he'd replied, but she'd caught the glint of pleasure in his hooded, dark eyes.

"Maybe it's not so astonishing," Rafe mused as they fell asleep in his big bed. "In his heart, I can't believe he'd really want you to go."

Lying beside him and gazing up through the skylight at the multitude of stars, Diana decided he was right. For several weeks following Buffy's wedding, she and Rafe had continued to see each other, sleeping together almost every night at his ranch or at Buffy's apartment.

When Diana *was* home at the winter ranch, where Josh remained most of the time because the lower altitude was better for his heart, she made a point of bringing up her lover's name now and then—just to get him used to the fact of Rafe's presence in her life.

In any event it was no secret that they were seeing each other. Word had almost certainly spread like wildfire the night of Buffy's rehearsal; within a day or two, everyone who was anyone knew all the details. Anyway Josh always had his sources. Reports of them together doubtless reached his ears on a regular basis.

Yet not once did he confront her about the issue, or even respond negatively when she mentioned the man she loved. He still nagged about her work on the reservation, of course. And occasionally she had the uncomfortable feeling he was biding his time, hoping she'd tire of Rafe if he didn't actively take her to task.

That feeling grew more acute on the several occasions Del visited the ranch while she was at home. She had the feeling he and her father were conspiring how to bring the two of them together. Any attempt to do that, of course, would be doomed to failure.

But there was a factor that offset Del's visits during those weeks that pleased and surprised her. Somehow, while her attention had been diverted to Rafe, Johnny's relationship with Josh had blossomed from initial suspicion and avoidance to the beginnings of a mutual friendship. More than once she found them together on the patio, talking and swapping information about horses, the Indian boy conversing like a sensitive adult with the crochety old man.

I hope the caseworker who promised to look into Johnny's situation can do something about it, she thought, watching them one afternoon. But in a way she was reluctant for the boy's sojourn with them to end. With his child's directness and simplicity, he had insinuated himself into her father's affections, supplying much-needed companionship Diana was unable to give in such unstinting measure, and defusing the Indian issue in a way she hadn't dreamed possible.

Mostly, those weeks were a peaceful, if busy, interlude for Diana at the clinic in Tuba City, where she was training a new nurse to take Buffy's place. But their mellow quality didn't last. One afternoon just after the clinic closed its doors, the phone rang while she was going over her records. It was Rafe, advising her he was bringing Mary Flatbow into the hospital.

"I'm no doctor but I'm pretty sure she's got cancer," he said, raising his voice over the static that threatened to disrupt their connection from the trading post at Magic Butte. "If it's progressed far enough, we may need to transfer her to an oncologist in Flagstaff."

"You know she wouldn't let me examine her that day at the clinic," Diana replied testily, devastated by the news. Somehow she would have to tell Johnny, and she wasn't looking forward to that.

"She'd been seeing a medicine man." His voice faded for a moment, then came over the line clearly again. "For people like Mary modern medicine is usually the last resort."

Mary Flatbow didn't appear to feel any remorse for neglecting her health when Diana met the helicopter at the landing strip. Several emergency-room techs had gone out too, and she didn't have time to do more than squeeze Mary's hand as the technicians transferred her to a gurney and wheeled her into the hospital.

As a member of the courtesy staff, Diana could enter the emergency-room cubicle while Mary was being examined and hooked up to an IV. She reported back to Rafe that Johnny's grandmother would be taken immediately to X ray.

"She probably has a tumor, but I don't suppose we'll know the extent of its involvement much before tomorrow," she said. "They'll have to do a complete blood work-up too. From the location of the mass I believe it's ovarian. Just pray it hasn't spread to her liver. If it hasn't, she probably has a fighting chance."

Going back down to the clinic, Diana dialed the Bureau of Indian Affairs social worker she'd contacted about Johnny's case. Without the stabilizing force of Mary in the home, she guessed, even Daisy and her pregnant mother might not be immune from James Fox's violence.

But it was well after hours and the phone rang in an empty office. Rafe appeared in the doorway and she put down the phone with a sigh, walked over with him to have a quick supper in the hospital cafeteria.

Before leaving for the night, they looked in on Mary again. She had responded well to her initial treatment, and was now settled in her room.

"You should have let me examine you that day at the clinic," Diana chided, frustrated in her desire to do something. "Or at least come into the hospital sooner."

Mary regarded her stoically. "I let Rafe bring me in so I can get stomachache medicine," she said. "Tell me, Dr. Diana . . . how is Johnny? When is he coming home?"

Under the circumstances, the date of Johnny's homecoming to Magic Butte was anybody's guess. "Johnny's fine," she assured his grandmother. "He and his cousin Joshua have become friends. But Joshua is sick too, and he needs Johnny's company for a little while. I'll bring him back to you soon."

A consultation the next day with the internist who was supervising Mary's case left Diana discouraged and depressed. Not pulling any punches because he was talking to a colleague, the thin, graying doctor outlined Mary's cancer in graphic terms, terming it inoperable. The family should seek a second opinion of course, he said. But he was certain a cancer specialist would concur. He held out a slim hope that the forty-five-year-old Indian woman might benefit from radiation treatments at the medical center in Flagstaff.

"I'd like to arrange for that immediately," Diana said. "If there's any problem with money, naturally I'll foot the bill."

The weary-looking doctor shook his head. "For once, money isn't the answer. Mary's refused to go. She's given her consent just for the first in a series of chemotherapy treatments that we can handle here. If I understand her correctly, she wants to return as soon as possible to some remote encampment across the Utah border."

Diana sighed. "I'm afraid you understood her all too well, Dr. Hamill," she said.

She was more than a little dispirited that night when she accompanied Rafe to a meeting at one of the Tuba City schools. Its subject was the relocation of Navaho families in response to congressional redrawing of Navaho and Hopi reservation boundaries several years before. It was a subject she'd first heard about since returning to Flagstaff at her father's dinner table.

Tonight, Rafe explained, members of the commission that had been appointed to carry out the congressional edict had called the meeting to explain why the recalcitrant Navahos had to move off the land they had always considered their home.

These families, Rafe told her, were the holdouts, the ones to whom pride of place meant more than the $60,000 each the government would spend to move them to small, modern frame homes on the former ranches not far from the Double Bar B.

"They don't understand why the Hopis can't go to the new area instead if they want more land," he told her under his breath.

Diana looked about at the solemn faces of the Indians who were crowded into rows of folding chairs in the school auditorium. These were dignified people, she knew by now, conservative people who didn't like change.

"The land where the government wants to move them isn't so very different from the area they live in now," Diana observed, glancing at the map that one of the men from the relocation commission was tapping with a pointer. "In fact, it's probably better for grazing. The houses would be better too. I don't know why they're so reluctant to go."

"Don't you?" Rafe patted her hand, belying the sharp question. "Would your father trade for the DeLillis property down the road from him? Or unprotestingly let officialdom move him up north of the peaks if he didn't want to go?"

"We own property up north of the peaks," Diana said. But she had to concede his point. She couldn't agree that she would prefer a hogan to a real house with separate rooms and plumbing and windows. Still, hogans have their distinct advantages, she thought, remembering the first night she and Rafe spent together.

She refocused her attention as one of the speakers from the commission said the period of voluntary relocation would soon end. Those Navahos who didn't comply with the order, he insisted, would be forcibly relocated by federal marshals. Predictably, an undercurrent of angry talk swept through the room. Yet she saw that some of the people present, though they were listening carefully, still didn't understand.

"There are so many problems here it could take a lifetime to solve them," she told Rafe sadly as they walked out at the meeting's end. "Mary, Johnny's mistreatment at the hands of James Fox, the bewilderment and disruption of so many lives just because somebody saw fit to redraw their property lines on a piece of paper."

Something about the look he gave her said he was sorry he'd brought her to the meeting at all. "The relocation isn't quite that simple," he said. "I hate to admit it, but the Hopi have a point too. Just don't try to be responsible for everything that cries out to be changed on the reservation. I don't. I just do whatever I can."

Buffy's apartment was an island of comfort at the end of a troubled day. They let themselves in with the key Buffy had given Diana with an injunction to make good use of it. I'm not sure we will tonight, she thought. I feel more like settling down in his arms for a good cry.

Instead, she decided to tell him Max's story, hoping against hope he might be able to refute it or at least help her find out the truth. Postponing the moment, she put on the kettle for tea. While Rafe lounged against the edge of the kitchen counter, watching her, she made an infusion of tea, brandy and honey, and poured it out in two flower-printed mugs.

I wish we were at Rafe's beautiful cedar house, she thought—far from the tangle of Indian problems and the dilemma of my father. We could sweat out all our worries in the sauna, build another juniper fire, lie looking up at the stars.

"It's all been a bit too much for you tonight, hasn't it?" Rafe asked, putting his arms around her.

"Maybe," she admitted. "The old legends are so beautiful, even when they're cruel. Why do things have to be such a mess today?"

"Maybe nobody ever really lived in heroic times, though we all like to dream about them," he speculated. "I wish I could keep this ancient culture fresh and mysterious for you—just tell you stories by the campfire after loving you half to sleep."

"But life isn't like that."

"No. It's not."

"Rafe..." Unbuttoning several of his buttons, she slipped her hands inside his shirt so that she could feel the beating of his heart. "The troubles out here and Josh's attitude...they're not the only problems on my mind tonight."

"Nothing wrong between us, I hope?"

"How could there be?" She stood on tiptoe to kiss him lovingly on the mouth.

Sipping her tea in the shelter of his arm as they sat side by side on Buffy's overstuffed couch, Diana related what Max had told her—the story of her mother's alleged affair with an Indian, the accident, the dark child born dead who wasn't Josh's baby.

Rafe's dark brows drew together. "If Josh Bailey has Navaho blood, and I know he does, mightn't the child have been his?"

"That's what I want to think."

There was a silence between them. "Have you discussed this with your father?" Rafe asked. "What does he say? Does he back up Max's crazy story?"

Diana felt a little foolish. "I haven't wanted to upset him," she admitted. "Probably I'm afraid, too...that he'll tell me Max is right."

Rafe's arm tightened around her shoulder. "Some of my relatives...in fact, several of the people you met at the Yazzies' encampment...knew your mother well. Yet they've never hinted..."

"Yazzie..." Now Diana's brow was furrowing. "Your mother was named Yazzie, wasn't she? Why didn't you tell me those people were your relatives? And another thing...why didn't they raise cain about us sleeping in the same hogan together?"

His mouth curving, Rafe gave her a squeeze. "You're right, they're conservative people and normally they wouldn't have allowed it. Under the circumstances, though, they didn't mind."

Diana stared at him. "What circumstances?" she said.

"I told them we were planning to be married soon."

"So they thought that we slept together."

He grinned. "In the most intimate sense of the word."

Later, as they were about to drift off to sleep, Rafe brought up the subject of Max's story again. "You said you were *afraid* it might be true," he whispered, his voice faintly raspy beside her ear. "If it is, would that make a difference between us?"

She didn't give him a hasty answer. "I guess you know it would make things a lot more difficult," she told him at last. "But as for changing anything—" she traced the dark seam of hair that ran from his chest to his navel "—you ought to know better than that."

Rolling onto his side, Rafe took her back in his arms. "I can't make the problems we face go away, darling," he said. "But I can love you...with all my being. I just hope it'll be enough."

Rafe was shaving and she was standing beside him at the sink, brushing her teeth, when the phone rang. It was a call from the Department of Public Safety, requesting his assistance in a helicopter search for some hikers who had gotten lost in one of the more remote reaches of the Grand Canyon. Depending on how things went, he might not be back by nightfall.

Before driving back to the ranch to check on Josh and Johnny, Diana stopped in to see Mary and say hello. She was just heading out again when one of the hospital's lab techs, an Indian, stopped her.

"You took Johnny Flatbow home with you so his stepfather wouldn't beat him anymore," the man said. "That was a good thing to do. I thought maybe you'd want to know, doctor... James Fox has been arrested for getting in a fight at one of the taverns in Flagstaff."

The news was like a goad to her. Though she deplored the incident, she couldn't help viewing it as a godsend. Driving straight into town without stopping at the ranch, she went directly to Del Cates's office. For Johnny's sake, it's time to swallow your pride and your annoyance with him, she thought.

It felt a little strange, asking his secretary to see him and wondering if he'd relay a message that he was too busy to grant her an interview. But she needn't have worried about that. A moment later, he was emerging into the outer office, stiffly inviting her inside.

"Well," he said, regarding her uncertainly across his desk. "What prompted this visit? The last few times I've been at the ranch, you've barely had time to say hello."

The worst thing that can happen is that he'll turn me down, she decided. "I need your help, Del," she said. "I want your boss to throw the book at an Indian who was arrested in a tavern brawl last night."

Leaning back in his chair, Del gave her a puzzled frown. "I thought you were all fired up to help Indians, not put them in prison."

Succinctly she related the story of Johnny's injuries and her concern for the safety of the other family members. "Mary and Daisy won't talk," she conceded. "But I think I can persuade Johnny to testify."

"You're telling me the abuse of the boy took place on the reservation? That's out of our jurisdiction."

"I know. But couldn't it be considered as an aggravating factor in the battery case?"

Del shrugged. "I suppose I could talk to the boy."

Clearly he was less than enthusiastic about pursuing the matter, and she thought she knew why. "Okay," she said, getting to her feet, and picking up her purse. "I get the message. I just never thought you'd hold a grudge if I fell in love with somebody else."

"Oh, hell..." Coming around the desk, Del detained her. "I've been in love with you for years and you know it, Diana. Mostly I've held my tongue since this thing with Rafe Marquez got started, knowing how headstrong you can be. I guess I've been hoping it would end, and eventually you'd come back to me."

"It isn't going to end," Diana blurted. "I'm going to marry him."

His face blanched. "You can't do that!"

Del's voice held more than the despair of a rejected suitor. Her heart constricted. "Why can't I?" she asked, suppressing a thin wave of apprehension.

Del ran his fingers through his hair. "I don't want to be the one to tell you. You'd always hold it against me...think I did it out of spite."

I don't want to hear this, Diana thought. I want to walk out of here and never speak to you again. "Tell me," she insisted, corraling her fear.

"All right. I talked to Max when I was out at the ranch last week, and he told me the story about how your mother died, about the dead baby she bore her Indian lover."

Her cheeks hot at Max's gossiping outside the family, she felt her fury at Del rising too. "I already know that story," she snapped. "It doesn't make any difference."

"You don't know all of it." Del regarded her steadily for a moment. "Max told me the rest, the part he couldn't tell you. The man who fathered Ingrid Bailey's illegitimate child was none other than Rafe's uncle, the half brother of his Indian mother. His name is Ned Yazzie. And he still lives on the reservation today."

Ten

Weakly Diana leaned against the desk. She felt as if she'd been kicked in the solar plexus. For a moment, it was difficult for her to catch her breath.

"Sit down," Del urged contritely, his hand on her shoulder. "Please...let me get you some coffee or something."

"*No.*" The single word betrayed her anguish. With effort she pulled herself together. "I have to get out of here...handle this myself..."

I'm going to tell Josh, she thought, getting back behind the wheel of the Wagoneer. I can't avoid it now. I just pray to God it won't harm him, and that he'll tell me the truth.

Of course it wasn't really truth she wanted, but a denial—one that would let her live in peace with the man she loved. And if I don't get it? she asked herself, posing the most difficult question as she drove east on Santa Fe Avenue. Can I simply shut my eyes to the past and marry into the family of the man who did my father such deep injury?

It occurred to her that Del might have dealt the *coup de mort* to her love affair with Rafe. No, she thought, turning at the light and driving up the ramp toward the interstate. Not that. We love each other too much for it to end.

The thought of meeting Rafe in dark corners, carrying on a furtive affair, sickened her. But if the latest allegations she'd heard were true, Josh would never be able to tolerate anything more.

It struck her a few minutes later, as she pulled into the driveway of the Mount Pleasant Road house to pick up a few things, that her father had known about her and Rafe for some time—guessed, probably, what they were doing when they were alone together. If Rafe's uncle really did father my mother's child, why wouldn't Josh say something? she asked herself, leaning her forehead momentarily against the wheel. Isn't it so, after all? Or doesn't he know?

The phone was ringing as she unlocked the door. "We found the hikers," Rafe said. "But something else has happened...Mary checked herself out of the hospital this afternoon. Rather, I should say, she just walked out...wrapped in a blanket."

"My God!" Diana closed her eyes. "Where are you?" she asked. "How'd you know?"

"I'm in the DPS hangar at Flagstaff Airport. The head nurse on her floor told me what happened when I called for a condition report."

Suddenly exhausted, Diana sat in one of the fragile Chippendale chairs beside the phone. The image of Mary, ill with cancer and desperately in need of treatment, wandering out of the hospital and perhaps standing beside the road, trying to catch a ride back to Magic Butte, was almost more than she could take.

"Where is she now?" she asked finally. "Do you know if she got safely home?"

"Her medicine man drove her. You might as well know the whole story: she left on his advice after he came to see her at the hospital."

"That's crazy."

"Maybe. It's not very compatible with modern medicine, anyway. Diana..."

His voice held a question and she thought again how much she loved him, how impossible it would be now to live outside the haven of his love.

"Yes, darling?" she said.

"There's going to be a Blessing Way ceremony for Mary tonight in her hogan. Not the old-fashioned nine-day kind, but just one night. She left word she wants her family there... *all* her family, including Johnny, you and your father."

"You know that's not possible."

"I sent word that Josh is too ill to travel. I said you'd represent him."

There was a pause, as he waited for her to confirm his promise to the Indian woman. He wasn't saying so, but she got the impression that the presence or absence of family members might seriously affect the ceremony's outcome in Mary's eyes.

"Of course I'll be there," she replied, pushing down her own personal concerns. "Where shall I meet you?"

"At your father's ranch? We have to pick up Johnny too."

"That would create problems. I'm on my way out there now...I'll get Johnny and meet you at Tuba City. I'll need my car out there tomorrow anyway."

"All right, if you'd prefer." There was an echo of disappointment in his voice, as if he'd lost another round in a very important battle.

I won't be able to tell him what happened today, she thought, repacking her little duffel bag and going back out to the car. At least, not until after Mary's ceremony. Yet she was aching to share the burden of Del's allegations with someone, longing most especially for Rafe's comfort and support.

It was as if her dark-haired lover could read her mind when they met at the Tuba City airstrip. With a frown, he settled Johnny into the chopper's back seat and strapped him in. A moment later, he was facing her and taking her into his arms.

The chopper's blades were turning slowly, churning up enough noise that they couldn't be overheard. "What's wrong?" he demanded, holding her a little way back from him and searching her face.

"I'm worried about Mary, I guess," she answered, hoping he wouldn't press her.

He didn't for the moment, though she could sense he didn't accept her answer as the complete truth. "Life was much simpler for you before we met again, wasn't it, Diana?" he asked.

"Probably."

Just never doubt that I love you, Rafe, she added silently—no matter what the future holds.

Rafe set the chopper down some distance from the trading post at the foot of a frowning brown butte. There wasn't a tree in sight. The little cluster of hogans, all of them the traditional wood and mud variety, was surrounded by dusty, out-of-date automobiles and pickup trucks. Dogs barked and several brown-skinned children ran through the cloud of dust kicked up by the chopper to welcome them. She saw Johnny's mouth curve in the beginnings of a smile.

Earlier, he'd been in tears. In the Wagoneer on the way to Tuba City, she'd shouldered a parent's responsibility and tried to explain about his grandmother's illness. Stoic at first, the boy had suddenly sobbed and allowed her to draw him within the comfort of her arm.

Now, with a child's facility for compartmentalizing unhappiness, he gave a slim but heavily pregnant woman who was probably his mother a quick hug and ran off to play with his friends.

Her hand in Rafe's, Diana let him take her around for the necessary introductions. She didn't quail when he introduced her to the friendly but somewhat solemn and reticent adults as Mary's cousin, "the woman I'm going to marry."

I hope to God he's right, she thought, and wished she had his confidence at that moment.

Though she'd brought her medical bag, they wouldn't let Diana examine Mary or even see her until preparations for Blessing Way, one of the oldest and most revered Navaho ceremonies, were completed. Somebody produced an illegal six-pack of beer from the back of a truck and they stood around, leaning against the trucks and drinking it, not talking much and waiting for the afternoon portion of the ceremony to begin.

Standing there, sipping her slightly warm beer and aching from the pain of what Del had told her, she tried to concentrate on the ritual ahead. On the way out in the chopper, Rafe had told her what to expect.

"It won't seem very scientific to you," he'd warned her. "And it isn't, of course. But medicine men study many years in order to practice their art. Not only are they highly respected for their skill at setting broken bones, for example; they also have the instincts of a psychologist and mystical abilities of a priest to heal the soul. It might help, *querida*, if you looked at tonight's proceedings through your spiritual, Navaho eyes."

I almost wish I could believe in charms and potions, she thought ruefully, looking at Rafe. My soul is feeling a little sick today. I'd beseech the Indian gods of Mary's ceremony to intervene on our behalf. If Del's story turns out to be true, I don't know what I'm going to do.

It was almost supper time when a tall, gangly youth named Joe Ectilly called them into Mary's hogan. Rafe squeezed her hand as they separated and went to sit on opposite sides. Preening a little, Johnny took his place beside Rafe and the other men while Daisy and Rozanne Fox moved over to make a place for Diana between them.

Gradually her eyes adjusted to the dim and smoky light, her own problems temporarily forgotten as she looked about her. Of necessity, the fire had been removed to one side of the hogan, and rags of blue smoke drifted at an angle to the smoke hole overhead. A bowl of water had supplanted the fire in the exact center of the dwelling, as Rafe had said it would, to represent the hole of emergence through which the Navaho people had entered the upper world.

Beneath the bowl was the first real sand painting Diana had ever seen, precise and exquisite with its soft reds, yellows and blues that were almost gray, its creamy-white ground. She recognized the traditional rainbow design and stylized, semiabstract representations of Indian gods from illustrations she'd seen in books.

Prayer sticks had been placed along the rainbow's softly striated colors. On one side of the painting, as if she intended to merge with it, a sober and withdrawn Mary sat wrapped in a gray and brown blanket. Across from her, the medicine man sat facing the hogan's entrance, his proud, wrinkled face half-lost in the indigo shadows, his gnarled hands resting on lean shanks.

When everyone was seated, the old man slowly raised his head. He began to sing in a thin, high voice, sprinkling what Diana guessed was corn pollen on the magic figures of colored sand. The unintelligible chant, musical but with guttural inflections and keening, almost wailing accents, touched off waves of shivers over her skin. My heritage, she thought, looking across the dim, crowded hut to meet Rafe's eyes. Something in me recognizes that—even if this runs contrary to all my experience and training and I have no living memory to support what I feel.

Actual treatment began, with the medicine man rising to touch parts of the painting with sacred meal and then corresponding parts of Mary's body, concentrating on the affected areas. He anointed her forehead with meal and placed a small amount of meal in her mouth.

While others in the hogan remained silent, concentrating intently, Mary also began to chant. Her voice

was a low contralto that somehow rent the heart in the
credulous counterpoint it wove to the old man's song.
Bits of sand were brought to her from the painting also
and touched to various parts of her body.

Finally, when Diana was stiff from her prolonged,
silent posture on the hogan's earth floor, Mary arose.
Several men stepped forward to destroy the sand
painting and carry the sand away. Rafe held out his
hand to her, and they went out together into the early-
evening light.

During the afternoon healing, several things had
happened. Quite a few more people had arrived. A
wide circle of trucks and cars had been drawn up
around Mary's hogan. Inside the makeshift enclosure, a large bonfire had been laid, ready to light.
From beyond it, the sound of snapping cedar trees and
the smell of cooking meat, beans and coffee drifted to
their nostrils.

They ate with Johnny and Rozanne and several
other people Rafe said were more distant relatives of
hers. Nearby some young men were gambling over a
dart game in the failing light. One of the women was
nursing a baby, quite matter-of-factly, without either
modesty or pride. When the child had finished suck-
ling and was seated upright on its mother's lap, Diana
thought its solemn eyes sparkled like jet in the wavering light.

"The rest of the sing will be outdoors, because the
hogan is too small to accommodate all these people,"
Rafe told her as the meal ended. "We'll be able to sit
together. It's going to get cold ... I'd better get our
jackets out of the chopper."

The night ceremony began with the rising of what
was considered to be a propitious star. Diana leaned

into the curve of Rafe's arm as the musicians entered
the enclosure first, playing their primitive collection of
instruments. Suddenly the drab encampment was
transformed to a scene of stark beauty as they touched
off the huge bonfire, causing flames to shoot up into
the night and sparks to fall like rain. Light flickered
over aristocratic, high-cheekboned faces, glinted off
heavy handwrought silver, illuminated the whites of
intent obsidian eyes.

Dancers entered the circle of trucks and bodies,
yelling and leaping, their skin chalky with traditional
white clay to represent the Navaho conception of the
yei, or gods. Their bodies shimmering in the waves of
heat from the fire, they made a double circuit around
it, finally approaching it and burning what looked like
decorations of down or feathers from their ceremo-
nial wands.

"This is the eagle ceremony," Rafe whispered as the
slim young men shuffled in sinuous motion, winding
between the fire and the onlookers as they sang a
querulous chant. "They complain to the gods of
Mary's illness. No matter how Blessing Way is var-
ied, this chant always plays an important part."

At the end of the eagle dance, Mary came out of her
hogan and sat down on a blanket. She looked worn
and tired, her face almost gray in the firelight. Diana
saw Johnny, across the fire from them now, gazing at
her with awe and sudden awareness of what the ceremony was all about.

"*Hu-hu-hu*-hu!" Another *yei* dancer in a blue mask
stepped to the forefront, shaking what Rafe said was
called a "groaning stick." Its thunderous sound rose
above the snapping of the fire and the chant of the

other dancers, echoing off toward the butte in that vast, open place.

As the night wore on, one dance followed another, sometimes with long waits in between, and it grew quite cold as the desert sky filled up with stars. Diana huddled against the man she loved, hypnotized by the virtuosity of the dancers' footwork and their angular grace.

For the first time she was able to appreciate the emotional benefit of ritual, not only for a patient but for his family and others, to understand fully the benefit of loving human support. For Mary, she realized it had probably already been too late when she finally consented to let Rafe take her to the hospital.

Mary had probably known that too, when she'd left the hospital that afternoon with her medicine man. In Diana's experience patients usually sensed the gravity of their plight. Maybe Mary was right to opt for this pageant with its incalculable benefits and time-honored history, she thought, aware that some of her colleagues back east might disagree with her. Maybe the healing was intended for the spirit anyway.

Several acts of magic followed, including the yucca trick with its insistent chanting, in which a yucca plant appeared to bud and bloom within a few moments' time.

"I performed that role when I was ten," Rafe whispered, when one of the *yei* dancers returned with a boy who was stripped and painted, wearing only a blue kirtle and moccasins. "In a ceremony for my mother, just before she died."

Though her eyes were heavy, Diana watched with fascination as the boy danced to the grown men's chanting, causing an eagle quill to rise in the basket he

carried so that it seemed to move in perfect harmony
with his footsteps. She tried to picture Rafe as a slim,
black-haired child with aristocratic Spanish features,
about to be orphaned, moving with skill among his
Indian relatives in the flickering firelight.

They slipped out soon after that, Rafe reminding
her that she needed to sleep if she planned to work at
the clinic in the morning. Across from them, Johnny
and some of the other children had already fallen
asleep.

Her hand held fast in Rafe's, they walked to a hogan at the far edge of the encampment, where earlier
they'd deposited their things. Quickly he lit the fire
that had been neatly laid for them, pulled together the
two cornhusk mattresses that awaited at opposite ends
of the single room and added several extra blankets.

Watching him, Diana remembered how he'd introduced her earlier as the woman he planned to marry.
Then she felt her tension return. I hope to God he was
right, she thought, because I don't think I can live
without him; but I won't know what to do, or where
to turn if Del is telling the truth. Though she longed to
tell Rafe what was bothering her, a part of her hung
back, urging her to forget what she'd heard in Del's
office, and to think only of her own needs and desires.

Quickly the matter was taken out of her hands. As
the fire blazed up, warming them, Rafe turned to her
and placed his hands firmly on her shoulders. "I want
to know what's wrong, Diana," he demanded in a
tone that would brook no resistance. "All evening
long, there's been a sadness in your eyes."

Caught, she didn't try to prevaricate. His first reaction to the tale she told was astonishment. "I don't

believe I'm hearing this," he said finally. "I have only one uncle . . . the old man who told stories that night by the Yazzies' fire. Do you honestly think he's the sort of person who would cuckold your father?"

"I don't know *what* to think," Diana replied miserably. "Lots of people have affairs with other people who are married. I just need to know the truth."

"And you want me to *ask* him?" Something in his voice warned her that was unthinkable.

"No," she said. "Not if you don't think it's right. I plan to ask my father . . . as soon as Mary's ceremony is over and I can get back to the ranch to speak to him."

A silence reverberated with unspoken thoughts. Rafe was regarding her with narrowed eyes. "Suppose he confirms what Del told you, even if it isn't true," he said finally. "Neither of us can be held responsible for an affair that supposedly took place between two other people more than twenty years ago. What do you propose to do about it?"

"I . . . I don't know."

Her words weren't what he wanted to hear. "Not good enough, Diana," he insisted, his voice tight with displeasure as it carried to a boy who, unseen by them, had just reached the hogan's shadowed entryway. "I have a right to know what kind of commitment I can expect."

She was at a loss what to answer. "I won't necessarily believe Josh any more than Del, if that's what you mean," she began. "I fully intend to get at the truth . . ."

Rafe cut her off with an oath. "Knowing my uncle as I do, I'm convinced Del's story is a lie, told with the sole purpose of separating us," he said angrily. "But you're wrong if you think the truth or fiction of this means a damn to me. Even if Ned Yazzie did sleep with your mother, I don't see why that should change things between us."

Tears were stinging her eyelids. "I don't want it to," she said, aching at the rift she could feel developing between them. "But you know how my father's always hated Indians. If your uncle is responsible for that—for shaming him and alienating my mother's affection—I can't blithely marry into your family, bring the nephew of her lover home to his dinner table..."

Outside the hogan, Johnny Flatbow had understood only a small and very crucial part of what they were saying. He was crying too, wiping fiercely at his eyes with grubby fingers.

A twig snapped under his feet and they were silent a moment, listening. But the boy didn't make any further sound.

"Try to understand," Diana urged, clutching at Rafe's arms. "Josh is old, and I'm all he has now. He's been a good father to me. I'd lose him if this awful story turned out to be true and I just forged ahead with my plans. But that wouldn't be the worst of it..."

"What would be the *worst of it*, Diana?"

She was too distraught in that moment to read him very well. "Breaking his heart," she answered. "Even if not to have you would mean breaking my own."

"No...you're wrong." Rafe's hands fell from her shoulders. "The worst thing would have been for us to get married before Del dropped his bombshell. Loyalty is not something I'm willing to negotiate with a wife. And I'm beginning to think you don't understand the meaning of the word."

It was as if a chasm had opened at their feet. She found herself looking at him across it, her heart sinking at the way his face seemed suddenly to be carved out of granite. Nearby, the two cornhusk mattresses awaited, but she realized they wouldn't be using them that night.

"Rafe..." she whispered, attempting one last time to reach him.

But he wasn't really listening to her. "Get your things together," he said harshly. "We're not staying here tonight."

Nobody was about when they emerged from the hogan. "We ought to make sure Johnny knows we're leaving," Diana reminded in a small voice. "Or at least check on him before we go."

"All right," Rafe agreed, his voice expressionless.

But Johnny was nowhere to be found. At first they thought he might have returned to his mother's hogan to sleep. But the small dwelling was empty except for Rozanne Fox's meager possessions—the usual collection of pots and blankets and clothing hanging from pegs.

Returning to the circle of trucks and the bonfire, which was now burning low, they learned that neither Rozanne nor Daisy had seen Johnny for nearly an hour.

"He woke up and wandered off..." Rozanne told them shyly. "When he didn't come back, I decided he was with you."

Stowing their things in the chopper, they split up to search the encampment on foot by flashlight. But there was still no Johnny—not even by the time dawn streaked the sky with a pale wash of grayish rose and the guests at Mary's sing started to head for home. But though many people left, quite a few remained behind to help them look for the boy in earnest.

"Maybe he took his pony and went riding up to the butte," Daisy suggested hopefully. But the pony was in its makeshift paddock, and they went on to other speculations over cornmeal mush and coffee.

By the time the sun was up, Diana and Rafe were in the chopper, flying in widening circles over Magic Butte while the friends and relatives who remained sought the youngster on foot or in their pickup trucks. But it was as if Johnny had dropped off the face of the earth; they couldn't find a trace.

"I'm going to call the reservation police and ask them to keep an eye out for him," Rafe conceded at last, setting the chopper down near the trading post. "I don't understand why this has happened. But I think we've got a missing-person situation on our hands."

Eleven

———

Two officers from the reservation police—a pair of darkly handsome young men in their official-looking uniforms—came to take a report. When they'd given what information they could, Rafe and Diana headed back toward the chopper.

"I promised Mary and Rozanne that I'd find him," he said, not quite looking at her. "You have your clinic this morning. I'll drop you off at the hospital."

The last thing Diana wanted at that moment was to be sidelined from the search. Somehow—she wasn't quite sure why—she felt responsible for Johnny's disappearance. But it was too late to cancel the morning's session. Even as they spoke, she knew mothers with babies were trundling toward Tuba City from outlying settlements in their husbands' pickup trucks.

"The clinic is only scheduled until noon," she reminded him as she climbed into the chopper and fastened her safety belt. "I know you're very angry at me, but I want to help find Johnny too. If it wouldn't be too much trouble, could you swing by Tuba City about noon and pick me up again?"

He didn't answer for a moment, and she thought he might refuse her. She couldn't know how tired and vulnerable she looked, with her hair mussed and dark circles that spoke of many hours without sleep smudging her eyes.

"All right," he agreed finally. "But maybe it won't be necessary. Let's hope by then we've found him."

That morning, Diana found the practice of medicine onerous for the first time in her life. Whereas she usually enjoyed dealing with patients, particularly the handsome, dark-eyed Indian children who attended the clinic, she chafed at her duties. Glancing regularly at her watch, she vented her impatience on the temporary nurse who had taken Buffy's place. Try as she would, she couldn't get her mind off Johnny, or stop going over the argument with Rafe in her mind.

Snatching up her things just before noon, she apologized for her irascible behavior and ran out to the airstrip. Rafe was just setting down. This time he didn't smile, or get out of the chopper to greet her. Instead, his dark brows were drawn together in an impatient frown. She'd barely taken her seat when they took off again, going up like an elevator, soaring to perhaps two thousand, five hundred stomach-churning feet in a matter of seconds.

"I take it you haven't found him yet," Diana said, not expecting an answer.

For the first day of the search, they were on their own. They couldn't ask the Department of Public

Safety to join them in looking for Johnny for at least twenty-four hours.

Tense with each other and irritable from lack of sleep, they headed back in the direction of Magic Butte, crossing and recrossing the same arid country, scrutinizing every wash and juniper bush until their eyes literally burned for relief.

There was no sign of Johnny anywhere, though the land was so barren that it would be difficult for a jackrabbit to hide.

"I called Josh and told him about Johnny's disappearance," Diana told Rafe after several hours, rubbing her temples.

His eyes intent on the ground below them, her lover didn't express any interest in Josh's reaction.

"He was very worried," she volunteered anyway. "He promised to let the reservation police know immediately if Johnny turns up at the Double Bar B."

Rafe turned to look at her then. "You think Johnny would have some reason to go back there?" he asked, raising one level brow.

She shrugged, longing to rest her hand on his knee but knowing that, just now, her touch wouldn't be welcome. "I don't know," she admitted. "But something strange has been happening...he and Josh have grown close. You could actually say they've become friends."

Rafe's dark eyes were incredulous. "And this is the father who hates Indians?" he said, a note of bitterness echoing in his voice.

This time, Diana didn't reply. They continued to scour the general area of Magic Butte without success until sundown, when they put down at the Flatbows' encampment again for the night.

Probably their curt manner with each other was noted by her Indian relatives and attributed to worry over Johnny's disappearance. Immediately upon landing, Rafe went in to speak to Mary and assure her they were doing everything they could.

"How is she?" Diana asked several minutes later as they sat down by Rozanne's fire to drink coffee and eat leftover stew.

"Awfully tired."

She didn't press him for details. Bone weary herself from nearly thirty-eight hours without sleep, she ate in silence and then walked with him to the hogan where their dispute had started the night before. Their backs to each other, they disrobed in the dark and bedded down to sleep on opposite sides of the room without even saying good-night.

The victim of restless dreams, Diana felt she was being pulled from the bottom of a well when Rafe shook her shoulder. It was still dark. "If you're coming with me, we'd better get started," he said in a low voice. "If not, there's someone at the next encampment who can take you back to your car."

Anger cleared the drowsiness from her eyes. "Just because I won't abandon my father before I know all the facts doesn't mean I don't care about Johnny," she snapped, shrugging off his hand. "Please don't speak to me about dropping out of the search again."

Packing flat Indian corn bread and a thermos of coffee, they hit the sky at dawn, to breakfast silently in the air as they flew back over Flagstaff to the DPS hangar. Diana insisted on accompanying Rafe into the olive-green corrugated metal building that stood at the weed-rimmed far reaches of the northernmost runway.

She drank more coffee, trying to energize herself as Rafe filled out another report and answered the rescue officer's questions.

"We'll get on it right away, Marquez," said Bill Landrum, that day's crew captain. "Think we should call Sky 12 from Phoenix to help?"

Rafe shook his head. "Not yet," he answered. "But if the weather changes..."

It was scheduled to worsen in the next twenty-four hours. Thunderstorms, possibly bearing hail, would be rolling in from the west by the following evening, and the rain was expected to be cold. We'll find him before then, Diana thought. We *have* to. If Johnny had stayed in the desert, she realized, the worst he'd get was a thorough soaking and a mild chill. But by the time another day passed, he could be anywhere. And at the higher altitudes...

She walked down with Rafe to the NOAA weather station at the airport terminal, watched and listened while the meteorologist on duty explained the expected weather patterns, and showed them the path of the coming storm on his computerized charts.

As they returned to the chopper, one of the DPS pilots ran out of the hangar to tell them a police report had come in. "The story of Johnny's disappearance has been on the radio," he said. "A rancher remembered picking up a boy of his description along the westbound interstate and called the state troopers."

"*When?*" Rafe asked urgently.

"That was yesterday afternoon."

He gave a heartfelt sigh. "We'll have to broaden the area of our search."

"At least we know what direction he's heading," Diana consoled as they took off again. "We won't have to check out the entire states of Utah and New Mexico."

"No." He was silent a moment, massaging the tendons of one shoulder. "But if he's hitchhiking, he could be in California by now, for all we know. I don't understand any of this . . . why he ran, what his purpose was. It's almost as if it had something to do with us, and the trouble we're having. But I know that's not logical at all."

It was the most he'd said to her in two days and she felt a glimmer of hope that his anger had subsided, though she didn't intend to push her luck.

"Somehow I feel he didn't go that far," she answered. "He would need a reason to leave so abruptly, without telling anyone. He's lived in this area all his life. That reason couldn't extend outside the boundaries of what he knows."

Two choppers and the added vigilance of the DPS rescue pilots, not to mention their ground support from the state police and local agencies, didn't seem to help appreciably in the search. *The only difference is that we've covered more ground,* Diana thought, as they joined the public service crew for a late meal of hot dogs and beans in the hangar's dayroom.

Over and over she reviewed what she'd said to Rafe about Johnny's reasons. *I just wish we knew what they were,* she thought. *Then we might have a prayer of finding him.*

Despite the fact that Rafe's ranch was only a few miles distant, they spent the night at the airport, drinking coffee and obsessively checking police reports. *If things were different between us, we'd prob-*

ably have gone to his place, she thought. But she had
to concede that he might have chosen the same course
of action anyway, wanting to be on hand in case a
positive identification came in, or someone phoned
with news of Johnny's whereabouts.

The two-man DPS crew, used to working twenty-
four-hour shifts, didn't seem to tire as the hour grew
late. Playing gin rummy with his assistant while he
manned the radio, Bill Landrum looked up at about
2:00 a.m. to offer temporary use of the hangar's
bunks. Reluctant to give in and sleep but so tired she
was almost seeing double, Diana accepted.

"You too, Marquez," Landrum insisted. "It's
gonna be a long, hard day at the stick tomorrow. You
can spare four hours to get some rest."

She felt slightly uncomfortable as they walked into
the rescue station's tiny, utilitarian sleeping quarters
together. Two neatly made-up bunks, a dresser and a
small bathroom met her eye. Taking off her belt and
shoes, she sat down on the edge of one of the cots and
rolled her head from side to side until her neck made
a cracking sound. Still her neck and shoulders ached
from the long, intent hours she'd spent in the chopper, surveying the ground, and she reached around
awkwardly to massage a particularly stubborn knot.

"Lie down, I'll rub it for you," Rafe offered, a
study in mixed emotions.

Trying not to seem too eager, she stretched out flat
on her stomach against the tightly tucked blanket. The
cot settled a little beneath Rafe's weight as he sat down
beside her. Then she was wincing with combined pain
and pleasure as he kneaded her shoulders with strong,
capable fingers, instinctively finding each knot and
tender, aching place. Just to have him touch her again

when she'd been feeling so isolated from him was a joy, and the easing of her stiff, sore muscles was added bliss.

But she didn't dare trust to the feeling.

"Better?" he asked after several minutes, staying his hands.

"Yes. Thanks very much." She kept her face turned into the pillow, unwilling to let him see how much she longed for him to take her in his arms.

"Well, good night then, Diana." He pulled up the woven cotton spread to cover her partway. A moment later, the springs of her cot creaked as he got to his feet.

"Good night, Coyote Man," she whispered, so softly that he couldn't hear.

Morning came and with it another day that was like a replay of the previous forty-eight hours. They widened the search again, extending it from Walnut Canyon on the east to the small town of Williams, and from just south of the peaks to the Mogollon Rim. Still there was no sign of Johnny. It was already half past four when they returned to base to take on fuel for the third time that day.

While Rafe went inside to check the latest reports, Diana paced beside the helipad, staring off at the distant San Francisco peaks, which were clearly visible from the high ground of the airport. The weather that had been predicted the day before was already moving in and the temperature was dropping. When it broke, she knew, the rain would be cold and she prayed Johnny was in a safe, dry place.

Suddenly she stared harder at the peaks, such an emblem of northern Arizona life that sometimes she hardly saw them at all. She was remembering a brief

conversation she'd had with the boy during his recent
stay at her father's ranch. In it, he'd described his real
father, a Hopi who'd believed strongly in the benev-
olent kachinas who were supposed to inhabit the ancient mountains.

His round, dark face very serious, Johnny had told
her he shared his father's beliefs. By this time she
knew the boy to be sensitive, highly imaginative and
self-reliant. If something was troubling him, she
wondered, something wrenching like his grandmother's illness, mightn't he run away to seek the comfort
of his ancestral gods?

Her certainty rose just by the feel of the situation.
"I know where he is!" Diana shouted as Rafe came
out of the green metal hangar. Forgetting herself, she
flung herself into his embrace.

Though he disengaged her arms from around his
neck, he held tightly to her hands. "Where?" he
asked, a look she couldn't read in his fathomless black
eyes.

Quietly he heard her out, glancing once or twice at
the distant mountains as she spoke. When she'd finished, to her surprise, he was inclined to agree that her
theory had a chance.

"We'll have to get moving quickly, with that storm
coming on," he told her. "If he's up there, I hope to
hell we find him soon. The low temperatures on the
peaks can drop below freezing at this time of year."

They took off, Rafe in his sheepskin-lined leather
jacket and Diana wearing a short red-and-black lum-
berman's coat of heavy wool he insisted she borrow.
The heavily wooded mountains, with their mantle of
ponderosa pine blending at higher altitudes into a
dense alpine forest of Douglas fir and white-stemmed

quaking aspen, made a difficult hunting ground. Rain was already blowing up as they approached and soon it pelted down, icy cold and mixed with hail, reducing visibility to a minimum.

Even if they could spot Johnny, Diana realized, looking at the thicket below as the light faded, it would be difficult—and dangerous—to set the chopper down. Yet she believed Rafe could do it if anybody could, with his innate skill and Vietnam experience in negotiating heavily wooded terrain.

Wearily scanning the steep slopes, she occasionally stole a glance in his direction. With an aching heart she noted his strong profile, lean jaw and tanned, capable hands. A man in a million, she thought—not for the first time. And I've probably lost him.

Yet what in God's name was she supposed to do? I haven't said I wouldn't marry him anyway, she rationalized, even if Del was telling the truth. But it would go against all decency and the debt I owe my father as his daughter to make any decision until I know the facts.

Still, she realized that if they didn't come to terms eventually Rafe would find another woman to warm his bed. And that didn't bear thinking about.

When it was fully dark, he turned on the chopper's searchlight and hooked up the infrared detection device he'd borrowed from DPS headquarters. Explaining that the gadget picked up differences in heat intensity, he switched on its small screen, which displayed a black-and-white video temperature map of the ground.

"Animals and people are warmer than the surrounding vegetation," he told her, his voice businesslike and impersonal. "If we pass over a fox...or a

Johnny Flatbow...you'll see an image on this screen that resembles a glowing lightbulb.''

It was getting late and their fuel was running low when Rafe picked up a bright object on the little screen. Almost simultaneously Diana spotted a movement in the brush below the trees on Mount Elden's upper slope.

"There's something down there...maybe an animal...but I don't think so," she told him with rising excitement.

Immediately he took them down for a closer look. Huddled under a blanket of leaves by a fallen log was a small, sodden figure. It was Johnny.

"Hold tight," Diana shouted, leaning out of the chopper as far as she dared. "We saw you. We're coming back to get you!"

His mouth a tight line of concentration, Rafe searched for a break in the trees and found one, woefully inadequate, a few hundred feet away. Skillfully he set the chopper down, narrowly missing the towering spikes of the trees.

Grabbing up a blanket and her physician's bag, Diana hit the stony, timber-littered ground running before he'd even cut back the engines. They reached Johnny at almost the same moment, sinking to their knees beside him. Rain and wind blew into their faces, stinging their skin like ice.

"Johnny!" Diana exclaimed, putting her arms around him while Rafe sheltered them with his body.

The boy's strong white teeth were chattering. "Rafe," he whispered, his voice hoarse and unrecognizable. "Miss Diana. I begged the kachinas that you would find me."

Shaking her head, Diana examined him as best she could without removing his clothing. Involuntarily Johnny cried out in pain as she probed his left leg. "It's broken," she said after a moment. "I'll have to administer a splint before we carry him back. Otherwise we might compound the fracture...and he could pass out from the pain."

Quickly Rafe retrieved a splint board from the emergency medical services kit he always carried. Her ungloved fingers awkward with cold, Diana worked as quickly as possible. Soon Rafe was wrapping Johnny in the blanket she'd brought and carrying him in his arms back to the chopper, through gusts of rain that felt as if it could turn to snow.

Their ascent through the tall trees in the dark was a harrowing one but Diana didn't really pay attention to that. Bending over Johnny in the back of the chopper, she was piling blankets over the shivering boy and giving him a shot for pain. A moment later she heard Rafe get on the radio, calling the DPS command to say that the search was over.

"We're on our way to Flagstaff Medical Center," he told them. "Over and out."

Meanwhile Johnny was watching her with bright, fevered eyes. "What made you run away like that?" she asked, half-afraid to hear his answer. "And how did you get out of the encampment, travel all the way south to the interstate without anybody seeing you?"

A small brown hand came out from under the covers, slipped into hers. "I hid in the back of someone's truck," he said. "They had a tarp over some sacks of feed and they didn't see me. When I got to the interstate, I just thumbed a ride."

"But why? Why did you go off without telling anyone...and to the peaks? Was it because your grandmother was sick? Did you go to find the kachinas to
pray for her?"

In the cockpit, she knew, Rafe too was waiting for
the boy's answer.

"No, it wasn't that." Johnny hesitated a moment.
"I left the fire and heard you and Rafe talking in the
hogan. You were mad at each other..."

"Oh, baby..."

"When you said Mr. Josh hated Indians, I thought
the fight was my fault," the boy confessed. "It made
me feel bad, and I decided to find the real kachinas,
not just their pictures in the sand painting. I wanted to
ask them to make things right."

Diana groaned. In the rearview mirror, she could see
Rafe's jaw tighten. He'll never forgive me for this, she
thought, not if we lived for a hundred years. Yet, at
the moment, Rafe's displeasure didn't seem to matter
as much as convincing Johnny things would be all
right. She realized to her sorrow how much Josh's
good opinion meant to the boy, who lacked a father
and had suffered such terrible abuse at his stepfather's hands.

"I shouldn't have said what I did about Josh," she
told him, holding tightly to his hand. "Maybe it was
true once, Johnny. But it's not anymore. And it never
applied to you."

In the emergency room at Flagstaff Medical Center, Johnny was treated for exposure. His hand digging into Diana's arm, he allowed them to set his leg
and apply a cast without much more than a whimper
or two.

Then the physician on duty was telling them that Johnny should remain at the hospital overnight for observation. Reluctantly Diana concurred. After seeing him settled in his room, she walked outside with Rafe.

"My car is still in Tuba City, where I left it several days ago," she told him hesitantly.

"I'll take you back, of course," he offered. "I'm going up that way anyhow, late as it is, to give his mother and Mary a firsthand account."

Though they'd just been through a highly emotional hour and a half together and concluded their search on a triumphant if bittersweet note, his tone was once more impersonal—much cooler than if she'd been a stranger. Achingly tired and longing to set things straight with him, she climbed aboard for the twenty-minute flight.

But she didn't push him to talk, viewing their differences as an impasse and uncertain how to go about changing it. Once she broke the silence to ask if it would be all right for her to pick up Johnny the next morning at the hospital and take him out to the ranch for a brief visit with Josh before he returned home.

"After everything that's happened?" he asked. "I don't see how that's appropriate."

"My father's been very worried about him too," she said. "I don't know how Johnny managed it, but he matters to my father very much. And I think the feeling is mutual. Johnny needs to see for himself that I was wrong, that Josh really cares for him."

Rafe didn't say anything for a moment. "All right," he agreed at last, though his disapproval was plain. "I'll pick him up about three, then...at your father's ranch."

She didn't demur, as perhaps he'd expected her to, and for several minutes they simply winged their way through the night in silence. I can't just let him go like this, not with so much bad feeling between us, she thought.

As they drew closer to Tuba City, where they would part, her urgency mounted. "I don't know how to say this..." she began at last, uncertain how to broach the topic they'd broken off so abruptly the night of Johnny's disappearance.

Rafe cut her off with an impatient gesture. "Don't worry," he said, misunderstanding her completely. "I won't make any demands on your father's hospitality. If you'll have Johnny ready at the appointed time, I won't even need to come up to the door."

"Darling, for God's sake..." Diana pleaded.

He shrugged off the hand she placed on his arm.

"Don't listen to me, then," she told him. "Even if that wasn't what I was thinking at all. I was only trying to say that maybe this accusation of Del's is all a mistake. We can at least find out, before..."

"No." The single word was uncompromising. "You've missed the point completely, Diana. I expect much more than a provisional commitment from you."

All too quickly, they were putting down at Tuba City, and she was stepping out of the chopper because she had to, lingering beside the helipad, her hair whipping in the breeze.

"Rafe...I love you!" she shouted over the din of the rotors, bereft at their impending separation.

He didn't answer. Instead, he simply lifted off into the night, leaving Diana standing there staring after a receding cluster of lights.

Twelve

When she appeared at the Double Bar B the following afternoon with Johnny, Josh simply opened his arms. Hesitant at first, Johnny hobbled across the study's priceless Oriental rug and came into them. While Diana watched, the youngster on his crutches and the old man in his wheelchair just held each other tightly for a moment.

"Well, Johnny...we're a fine pair of cripples, aren't we?" Josh said heartily, indicating a chair and footstool beside him. "Sit down, boy. You gave us all plenty to worry about. But I guess we can forget that, now that you're safe and sound..."

"You were worried about me, Mr. Josh?" Johnny asked, with wide, solemn eyes.

"Damn right!" The old man's voice took on a rough note. "We're friends, aren't we?"

Johnny cast a swift glance at Diana, who had remained standing in the doorway. She nodded, con-
firming what she'd told him the night before.

"Yes, sir," the boy answered, his somber features
breaking into a smile.

They don't need me right now, Diana thought, giving them one last look to memorize the scene as she
stepped out of the room. They'll want to talk horses,
and Johnny will want to tell Josh about his adventure. After Rafe comes to pick him up today, it's going
to be as quiet as a tomb around here.

Exhausted from their three-day search and a restless night, Diana knew she wouldn't be able to sleep
until after she'd seen Rafe and broached Max's story,
complete with Del's embellishments, to her father.
Unfortunately, she couldn't accomplish those things
in their optimum order. I'll be darned if I'm going to
upset these few hours Josh has with Johnny, she
thought, even if that means I don't have any answers
for the man I love.

Too upset to eat, she skipped the lunch that Josh
and Johnny shared under the sycamore tree and spent
the last shreds of her energy currying down her favorite saddle horse in the barn.

Rafe arrived for Johnny in the chopper precisely at
three. True to his word, he didn't approach the house,
but simply waited beside his craft.

In the hall a suitcase stood ready, filled with the
clothes and books that Diana had bought for Johnny
during his stay. Gravely the boy and Josh shook hands
and then hugged each other goodbye.

"You come back and see us, son," Josh told him,
suspiciously misty-eyed. "That horse you've been

riding needs the exercise. And you don't want that foal to grow up without you."

"No, sir!"

"C'mon, Johnny," said Diana, quietly taking his hand. "It's time to go."

There was a lump in her throat as she took Johnny outside to meet Rafe. I love you, Coyote Man, she told her tall lover silently as she handed him Johnny's suitcase. Why can't you help me wrestle with this problem instead of being so angry with me?

But nothing had changed since the night before and she knew it. The aching chasm she'd created between them with her uncertainty was still there; she could read his alienation in every line in his body.

"Well, Diana..." he said, turning back to her after settling Johnny and his crutches in the back of the chopper. "I guess this is goodbye."

Desperate, she swallowed her pride. "We're not just going to end it like this, are we?" she said. "After everything we've been to each other?"

Standing there in fresh jeans and a blue plaid shirt she hadn't seen before, he was the most beautiful man she'd ever known. But it hurt to look at the flint-hard quality of his eyes.

"What we had was already over when your commitment started depending on something outside ourselves," he answered, his deep, faintly rough voice biting off the words.

Pain twisted in her midsection. Turning away, he walked around the chopper and got behind the controls. Johnny waved as the overhead rotors began to spin faster and faster, stirring up clouds of dust and beginning to give off their familiar chopping sound.

Moments later she was shading her eyes against the storm of grit and dust as they lifted off, cutting away at a sharp angle toward the misty buttes of the reservation and Rozanne Fox's hogan. I've lost him, she thought, blinking back tears so Josh wouldn't see them streaking her face. And without him, nothing else matters in all the world.

Almost nothing else matters, she amended as she went back inside and saw the look on her father's face. Hunched in his wheelchair by the study window where he'd watched Johnny's departure, he'd never looked so old. Josh is going to be tremendously lonely without his "little Navaho brat," she thought—almost as lonely as I'll be without my Indian man.

"It'll be all right, Dad," she consoled, crossing over to give his good hand a squeeze. "Maybe the Flatbows will let him come back for a visit now and then."

"Maybe." Josh's hooded brown eyes searched her face. "I was watchin' him go, sugar," he said. "That was Joaquin Marquez's boy who came for him, wasn't it?"

"Yes," Diana said, afraid the single word would betray her heartache.

"He's a fine-looking young man. I can see why you're so crazy about him."

For a moment, she couldn't believe her ears. Then, "What are you saying?" she demanded, her voice full of pain. "I thought you didn't want your daughter mixed up with a half-breed."

To her astonishment, Josh confessed that he'd had a change of heart—brought on by Johnny's presence in his life and her own quiet insistence on taking people at their human value, a trait her mother had also possessed.

"In the beginning I was very much against your seeing him," he said. "And I guess that went on for quite a while. But even an old prairie dog like me can learn from his mistakes.

"Johnny was one of the best things that ever happened around here. So sober and respectful...so intelligent and proud...he just found a crack in that old shell of mine and walked right in.

"You brought him. And his being here made me look at what you were doing in a new way. I saw your mother in you, and her concern for people..."

"Oh, Josh..."

"Hell, honey, don't cry. I only want you to be happy."

They were still holding each other's hands, but now it was Josh who was squeezing hers. *Without Rafe, that's impossible,* she thought. *And when you hear what I have to tell you...*

"As for young Marquez," her father said, "I'll admit it, girl. I had my lawyer do a little checking. He's a fine, upstanding citizen...educated, well-off, with his father's deep concern for others. Since I got a good chance to look at him just now, I don't have any doubts on another score, either: he could sire you some mighty fine-looking babies to love."

At the overwhelming irony of what Josh was saying, Diana burst into tears. "They'd be half-breeds, Dad," she wept. "*Part Indian.* I thought that mattered to you."

Incredibly, her father's craggy visage rearranged itself in a shamefaced look. "I've got another confession to make, honey," he said, drawing her down to sit at his feet on the little footstool, as she sometimes had when she was a child. "I lied when I told you the Baileys didn't have Navaho blood."

Diana was speechless.

"I was ashamed of it," Josh went on, forming his words with difficulty as he always did when they were heavily freighted with emotion. "When I was just a kid, I saw how even part-Indians were shunned. Of course, things were different then. But I vowed people would never treat me that way. Your grandmother Delia was dead and folks forgot her, acted like Jane Tutman was my real ma. I just let them think so.

"Until that Navaho smashed into Ingrid on the road, running down Indians was just a means of convincing people I wasn't one of them. It got to be a habit, one I didn't bother to examine anymore. But it was like a canker... because I was really turning that prejudice against myself."

"But after the Navaho killed her..."

For a moment, Josh shut his eyes. "I finally *had* a reason. But it's like you told me, sugar... it wasn't enough justification to hate a whole people. Ingrid would have been the first person to remind me of that."

Diana dabbed at her eyes. "Why didn't you tell me before this?" she groaned. "Surely you must have known what it would mean..."

"I didn't realize what a fool I was being until Johnny got lost. When that happened, I had time to think about Ingrid too, and work my way through some of that hurt. Watching you and that Marquez boy just now, I could tell how much he means to you. But there's something I didn't understand... why the two of you were acting so funny... and why he didn't kiss you goodbye."

"Oh, Dad..." Grieving, Diana laid her cheek against his knee. "That's because we aren't going to see each other anymore."

"On my account?" Plainly, Josh wasn't willing for that to be the case.

She raised her gray eyes to his brown ones. "I think it's time I told you a story, Dad," she said.

Both relieved and miserable, Diana poured out the whole unhappy story Max had told her, adding Del's ironic twist.

"Hogwash!" her father exclaimed, adding a few more graphic terms. "That baby was mine."

With his good hand, he set the electric wheelchair in motion, gliding across the Oriental carpet to the desk and pressing the intercom button. "Max," he barked into the speaker when his foreman answered. "I want to talk to you. Now! Get your butt over here."

Diana was blowing her nose as a wary Max walked into the room.

"Diana says you told her Ingrid's second baby was fathered on the reservation," he said. "You hand Del Cates another line that the Marquez boy's uncle was responsible?"

Max swallowed. Then, "What if I did?" he asked, giving Diana a sidelong glance. "I had a damn good reason. I knew what she was doin' would break your heart."

Josh passed his good hand over his eyes. For the first time, perhaps, he was realizing how far those who loved him had gone to protect him. "I want you to get on the phone and apprise young Cates of the truth," he ordered, "before he tells that story to anybody else."

"Yes, sir!"

Behind Max, the study door closed with a bang. Diana turned back to her father. "This whole damn mess is mostly my fault," Josh was saying. "After the accident, when Ingrid was at the hospital, I was grieving and ashamed. I didn't want the doctor or anybody else to know I had fathered an Indian baby. Max made up that story, and I never set anybody straight. It was a sacrilege to your mother's memory, and I'm not very damn proud of it today."

By now, both father and daughter were crying together. "But why did Max have to resurrect it now?" she asked. "He and Del both made me think that if I married Rafe that it would kill you, or break your heart."

"Hell, how should I know? Misguided loyalty. And jealousy, I suppose. Max has worked all his life for somebody else, while Rafe Marquez, who grew up on the reservation, has his own spread and a business besides." He paused. "Can you ever forgive me, girl, for the heartache I caused you?"

With a sob, Diana put her arms around him. "I'm grateful that you finally told me the truth, Dad," she whispered. "But I'm afraid it's too late for Rafe and me...even if you'd accept him now."

Her desolation as she explained Rafe's insistence that her loyalty to him should have been unquestioning clearly wounded Josh to the heart.

"Go on upstairs and get some rest," her father suggested, sorrow giving way to some of his old determination. "After the past few days, you need it. Maybe your old dad isn't good for much of anything these days. But he's going to try and straighten things out for you."

Uncertain what Josh was planning and doubtful he could move Rafe in any case, Diana went upstairs and stretched out on her bed. Now that she knew what had really happened, she believed it was too late to mend things. Rafe had wanted her unwavering commitment no matter what the truth turned out to be. And, because of Josh, she hadn't been able to give him that while it could still have made a difference.

Her head full of the conversation with her father and all the events of the past few days, Diana didn't even expect to close her eyes. More tired than she realized, however, she sank almost immediately into a deep and motionless sleep.

She awoke stiff and groggy nearly two and a half hours later to the sound of voices and the whinnying of horses outside her window. Rubbing the sleep from her eyes, she got up to have a look in the waning light. Dumbfounded, she saw Rafe with a horse trailer behind his pickup, unloading four of his best quarter horses. Max and Billy Shaw were helping him, while Josh looked on from his wheelchair, a lap robe folded over his knees.

Not pausing to comb her hair or even splash cold water on her face, Diana raced down the stairs. Billy and Max were just leading the horses away.

"What's going on?" she demanded in bewilderment, looking from Rafe to her father and back again.

The look of hidden amusement on Rafe's face was hard to miss. All the hard pride and pain were gone from his eyes. The little crease beside his mouth was deepening again.

"Just a business deal," Josh said, casually answering her question. "Long as I'm straightening out this situation for you, sugar, there's no reason I shouldn't make a profit."

Diana was as baffled as ever. *"Profit?"* she echoed, unconsciously poising one hand on her hip. "What do *you* have to say about this, Rafe Marquez?"

Rafe shrugged. His black eyes had a wicked gleam. "Just that I was on my way back from Magic Butte when I got an emergency call over the DPS radio. It was your father. He accused me of sleeping with his daughter, and demanded I do the decent thing."

Incredulous, she turned to face Josh. "You did *that*?"

"In so many words."

"But the horses . . ."

Try as he would, Rafe couldn't keep from smiling. "A down payment on the traditional bride price of twelve," he said. "I wasn't in a position to argue. Besides, it wouldn't be right for one Navaho to cheat another."

So Josh had told him everything. Unwilling to trust to her happiness, Diana stood there beaming at the two of them and hugging her arms.

"Aren't you going to say something?" Rafe insisted, his voice full of love. "Come here and kiss the man who's agreed to make an honest woman of you."

He held out his arms. Throwing Josh a look of pure gratitude, Diana went into them, to be crushed against her lover's hard, tall body. On hers, his mouth was balm for every hurt their estrangement had caused as he kissed her thoroughly and fully, his tongue claiming her soft depths.

Urgently her hands pressed the sculpted muscles of his back and shoulders. Please, she thought, her love for him overflowing, tell me this isn't a dream.

With a sigh he drew back from her a little, giving himself a moment to recover, she guessed. "I've spent the past four nights in hell," he whispered. "That's just a taste of what I have in mind for you."

A moment later, Josh coughed and remarked to the world at large that it was getting a little chilly out there by the corral. Laughing and twining one arm about her lover's waist, Diana walked beside him as he guided her father's wheelchair into the house.

Dinner that night was a cordial affair, with Josh and Rafe carrying on most of the conversation while Diana looked at both of them with love. She learned that Josh planned to give eight of the horses to Rozanne Fox, to help her pay for a divorce, if she wanted one, and assure her family's future. Further, Diana's father said, he planned to throw his considerable clout behind the prosecution of James Fox, so he wouldn't return to hurt Johnny again.

"The boy's mother will have her hands full caring for a newborn and for his grandmother in the near future," he said. "Rafe has promised to arrange for Johnny to come back here for a while and attend school."

"Between the two of us," Rafe added, "we plan to make certain Mary stays as comfortable as possible. She won't want for anything."

As the hour grew late and the two men she loved lingered over their cigars and brandy, Diana realized that her father must have invited Rafe to spend the night. I suppose that means we won't be able to sleep together, she thought. But she was far too grateful for the way things had turned out to complain.

By eleven, Josh was abed and Rafe had gone off to shower in the guest room that had been fitted up by Mrs. Purdy with fresh sheets and towels. Slipping down under her own covers in her wisp of a nightgown, Diana turned out the light.

A moment later, her door softly opened. "Darling," she whispered as Rafe found her in the dark.

He was barefoot, wearing only his jeans with the waistband snap already unfastened as he took her in his arms.

"I'm wild with wanting you," she admitted breathlessly, melting at the presence of his hands on her body. "But do you think we should...sleep together here?"

Faintly she could see the little line quirk beside his mouth as he eased the thin straps of her nightdress from her shoulders.

"Let's not start a tradition of wearing clothes to bed," he murmured, lightly kneading her breasts. "It was your father who told me where to find you. Anyway, don't forget...my Indian grandfather taught me to seal every bargain."

He took off his jeans. His caresses lighting little bonfires in her blood, Diana made no further protest. She shed her nightgown completely, unwilling to wait for any sweet, slow initiation. After the emotional pain of being at odds with him, she longed for an avalanche of fulfillment, the deep thrust of him within her body.

Through the language of touch, Rafe let her know that he felt the same way. Opening herself to him like a well, she drew him into the ultimate intimacy of her embrace.

How long they tangled there between the sheets of her childhood bed, erasing the last traces of hurt between them, Diana couldn't have said. She only knew that their release was the most profound she'd ever experienced, even in his arms.

We'll always be a part of each other, she thought, the heat of satisfaction flooding her body. It's as if he's married us already with the force of his love.

Quietly, she cuddled with her tall, bronze-skinned man in the too-small bed, still marveling at the circumstances that had brought them together in her father's house.

"How did Josh convince you to give us another chance?" she asked, tracing the dark seam of hair that marked his flat midsection.

Rafe kissed her tousled hair. "He told me he'd raised a fiercely loyal daughter who'd tear her own heart out before doing anything to hurt him," he said softly. "When I married you, he pointed out, that loyalty would be mine. He asked why I didn't admire you for it, instead of walking away."

Bless Josh, Diana thought, sending her father silent thanks. "And you answered..." she prompted, curious to know everything that had transpired between them.

The man she was going to spend the rest of her life with gave her a little squeeze. "I told him I didn't have a good reason, considering how much I love you."

Diana shook her head. "All those horses...I'll have to make it up to you, darling. I promise you one thing: you'll never have to deal with uncertainty from me again."

"I'm glad to hear it." Turning on his side, Rafe came back into her embrace. "Just the same, I plan to make sure of that. Josh needs a grandchild. And ever since you brought up the subject by the corral that night, I've been thinking how nice it would be to make a baby with you. What do you say we try to put a more permanent seal on our bargain tonight?"